Contents

Frontispiece
    The Shortest Day..1

When we are young...
    The Daisy-Chain..5
    Hide and Seek..7
    Poohsticks...10
    Lime House..12
    Donald and the Zligs..14
    Castle Marigold...17

Are you safe at home?
    Crackers...20
    Product Recall...23
    Tea and Cake..26
    Trapp..29
    Celandine..32
    The Cold Caller...34
    Broken Wing...37

Once upon a time...
    The Sparrow and the Glove......................................40
    The Three Ducks...42
    Going to the Dogs...45
    The Clockmaker..48
    The Shepherd and the Princess..................................58
    The Woodcutter and the Princess................................61
    Some Day...63

Meanwhile, in town...
    Taking off...66
    Breakfast Time..68
    Tunes from a Tin Whistle..71
    The Cares of the World..72
    Mustard..74
    How to Write a Poem...76
    Sausages...78

Away with the Fairies

fifty-five fantastical fables and a frontispiece

Oliver Barton

Copyright © 2022 by Oliver Barton

All rights reserved. This book or any portion thereof may not be reproduced or used in any manner whatsoever without the express written permission of the publisher except for the use of brief quotations in a book review or scholarly journal.

First Printing: 2022

ISBN 978-1-7391589-2-7

The Deri Press
27 Brecon Road
Abergavenny
Monmouthshire
NP7 5UH
UK

oliver.barton@talktalk.net
www.musicolib.net

Tall tales from the pub
- Duck's Dream 82
- St John and the Maiden 85
- Fish and Chips 87
- The Milkmaid 91
- Revised Version 94
- The Museum of Monstrosities 97
- Emmenthal Crackers 100

The animals know...
- Pastures New 108
- Nibbles 111
- A Glorious Dawn 114
- Meeting Mother 117
- Three Jiltings and a Civil Partnership 120
- How I met my wife 122
- Fowl Play 126

We are not alone...
- The Gadfly 129
- Tunnel Vision 131
- The Tree House 133
- Tarquin 136
- Genome 138
- The Presence 141
- Going on 145

The Third Age
- Ants in the Pants 149
- Pontin 152
- Single Malt 155
- Something to Do 157
- Don't Count Your Chickens 160
- Home To Go To 164
- Pink Bells 165

Frontispiece

The Shortest Day

And on the sixth day, God created man in his own image, and behold, he was tired after all the creating of the previous five days, and decided to knock off early. Even though the seventh day would be a rest day anyway, he felt he deserved the evening off. He climbed Mount Sinai to look over his work – the earth, sun and stars, the plants, fish, birds, animals, creeping things and man, not to mention day and night – and reckoned it was pretty good. An evening feast of ambrosia and nectar, an early night, and a lie-in on the morrow. That was just the ticket.

But God was not alone. He had Mrs God to consider.

'That was your shortest day yet,' she said as he came in. 'I'd have expected you to be working late, this being the last creating day and all, and with such a lot on the to-do list.'

God was about to protest that this was because his planning was second to none, as indeed he was second to none, but Mrs God wasn't finished.

'It's not as though you're omnipotent, whatever you may say in the blurb. You make mistakes. How about that tilt in the earth's axis? And those tectonic plates – I heard you had to hammer them home because you hadn't measured properly, and there are fault lines all over the place. They'll cause tears in the future, you mark my words. It's bad planning, sloppy, careless.'

God wanted to explain that he was trying out a new metric system of measurement instead of the old confusing cubits and that he got momentarily muddled, but she was unstoppable.

'Are you sure you've created everything? Have you created light?'

'You can see I have,' God began.

'Well, what about rock pools, aardvarks, Tyrannosaurus rexes, amoeba, the Blorenge, what of them?'

'Yes, yes, yes,' cried God. 'I think I have. It's difficult to say, until Adam actually gives them names.'

'Why don't you write these things down? You should have a check list.' Mrs God was not going to leave it alone.

'I do,' said God. 'I have a tablet. Two tablets. Samsung Galaxy. I use them. None of that pen and paper stuff. It would blow away in the hurricanes and things. It's a dangerous job, creating. You don't know the half of it.' God was patting his robes. He looked worried. 'Where are my tablets? Where did I put them?'

Mrs God was pouring out cups of tea. 'There you are. You may have a check list on your blessed computer things, but do you ever look at it? Oh!' She sighed. 'Don't tell me you've lost them.'

God looked frantic. His beard trembled in frustration. 'I know I had them. I was on Mount Sinai having a last look round, and I know I had them then. I was just sketching out some ideas for a few commandments to keep the fairies in line. Oh God!' He stopped suddenly, mouth and eyes wide open.

Mrs God cut a slice of Devil's Food cake and tutted. 'If I've told you not to take your name in vain, I've told you a hundred times. So you've left your computer things sitting on this Earth for anyone to see. That'll blow the gaffe on a supreme deity, won't it! They'll be able to read all your correspondence with Planet Control, and I hate to think what else. You'll be in big trouble.'

'Never mind that – it's not really a problem – I can turn the tablets into stone so they become non-operational. It'll only take a very minor miracle. And I've got a backup of my data. In cloud storage? Haven't I? I must have. Mustn't I? Oh, I don't know.' God collapsed into an armchair and smote himself on the brow. 'No, no, no, no, no,' he muttered. 'No, it's not the tablets that are the problem. Mrs G, I'm ruined'.

Mrs God sipped her Lady Grey and gazed sadly at him over her glasses. 'What is it now?' she sighed.

God looked at his hands, outstretched before him. 'What can I not do with these?' he asked rhetorically. 'I create a world in six days. Not many Gods can do that. And then I do this. I was so pleased with myself. It felt so good.' He turned tired, world-weary eyes upon his spouse, and reached out abstractedly for the sugar bowl.

'It's like I've created a chess-board,' he said. 'A chess-board and chess men, the table and chairs, the room to play it in. Even created the rules. And then I forget to create the players.'

Mrs God was all attention now. 'You mean... you can't mean...'

'Yes,' said God, and his divine lip quivered as a tear rolled down his cheek. 'I forgot to create the Fairies.'

There was a terrible silence, broken only by the clink of stirring tea.

'I was so pleased with my man. I thought, I can finish early! How's that for cool! So I rushed woman through and reckoned I was done. And there I was, all the men and women set up for entertainment and game playing, and I forgot to create the Fairies to play with them and run the place.'

'Can't you go back and do some overtime?'

'No, my dear. I've wrapped up Day Six on Earth. There's no going back. Union rules.'

'You are a prize idiot, God,' Mrs God stated bluntly. 'They'll never let you create another world.'

She watched God sink into the depths of his chair. He looked so forlorn, her heart went out to him. 'Can I get you a nectar and tonic, love. Pick you up a bit. There must be something you can do.'

'All I can do,' God said, 'as I see it... All I can do is... Is damage limitation, I suppose. I could sow a few myths in the ether, so that men *think* that Fairies exist. Yes. That could do it.' He was warming to the idea now. 'Ever-watching, vengeful, retributive Fairies, who are infinitely more important and powerful than themselves. There's an outside chance men will believe in them and will behave themselves, and won't get any fancy ideas about free will or nonsense like that.'

Mrs God handed him a tall glass with pink bubbling liquid in and a small paper umbrella. 'And if they don't?'

God pondered. 'There's a remote possibility they might romanticise them, I suppose, picture them in tutus, playing with flowers and sunbeams, but I don't think it's likely. No, I reckon it's the ideal clever solution. Efficient and cost effective. And in fact it's saved me a deal of arduous creating. It could catch on, you know, Mrs G.'

'Some hope,' said Mrs God. 'You've messed up good and proper. Shall I turn the tele on? It's the final of Strictly.'

When we are young...

The Daisy-Chain

The kids say she is a witch, so curmudgeonly is she. Her thin lips, pursed like a circumflex, snap out criticism and disapproval. If the sun shines, we will pay for it later. Supermarket food is tasteless, the independents too expensive. The local park is all dog poo. The council is incompetent. There are no proper winters any more. Other people are completely self-obsessed. Children are rude. Goods are shoddy.

It was not always so. Aged ten, Doreen was a flaxen-haired, bouncy bundle of joy, who would skip rather than walk, and thought snails were little people with caravans. She would sit in the meadow, humming tunes quietly, and make daisy-chains in the long, sun-sweet afternoons.

One day, leaning against the foot of an ancient oak, she thought she heard a cry from the ground beside her. 'Help!' it seemed to say. 'Help!' All she could see was a small hole at the base of the tree, perhaps made by a mouse or a shrew.

She put her head down close, and said 'Hallo! Who's there?'

'I'm stuck down this hole, stupid. Help me out,' the voice said.

Doreen tried to reach into the hole, but it was too small for her hand. She pushed a stick down, but all it produced was a tornado of screams and invective from below.

If only I had some string, she thought. An idea struck her. 'Listen,' she said. 'If I drop the end of my daisy-chain down, could you hold on, so I can pull you up?'

'Anything, anything!' came the voice. 'Just get on with it.'

So she fed her daisy-chain into the hole, flower by flower, until the voice cried 'Got it! Now, gently, gently.'

She pulled the daisy-chain out as smoothly as she could, to an accompaniment of obscenities that she was far too nice a girl to understand. After an age, a tiny pair of hands appeared, clinging on to the end daisy, and a tiny head, and a tiny body. With gossamer wings.

'Why!' cried Doreen, 'You're a fairy!'

'And you're a human. State the obvious, why don't you,' said the fairy. 'And while I am, of course, indebted to you, it is expressly forbidden for a human to look upon a fairy, and so I'm obliged to put a curse on you. Sorry, child. Regulations. It's this current régime. You humans don't have a monopoly on imbecile governments.' With which, the fairy flew off.

And from that moment, Doreen was cursed. She saw how the oak tree was rotting. She heard the whine of the tractor, not the song of the skylark. She saw mould and canker and discord where before there had been sweetness. She realised her mother's custard had lumps in, and how she smelled of cigarettes. From that day onwards, she saw the worst in everything and everyone.

And fifty years later, she still does, and the children call her a witch. She lives alone. In Doreen's eyes, her cottage is damp, her landlord a swindler, her roses have blight, her cat has fleas, and the drains smell.

She works in accounts for an international company, and terrorises the workforce with her pettiness and acidity. Even the division manager can only claim expenses between 3 and 3.30 on alternate Tuesdays, and is made to feel an inch high when he does.

One evening in her parlour, she looks up from the newspaper she is reading, with its reports of how individuals, the economy, the country, the world are all doomed in many dire and irreversible ways thanks to 'other people', and there is the fairy standing on the table before her. It looks exactly the same as fifty years previously, which is more than can be said for Doreen.

'There's been a régime change,' says the fairy. 'New regulations. Curses are now for a max of five years, – five years, I ask you! – and anyway, nobody cares if humans catch sight of fairies any more.' The fairy tuts fiercely. 'Place is going to the dogs, in my opinion. Standards slipping. Still, there you are. You're free. Curse lifted as of now.'

Doreen thinks for a moment. Then 'No, thank you,' she says. 'I realise I enjoy being a grumpy old woman. And I don't want charity from anyone. As far as I'm concerned, the curse stays.'

The fairy pouts. 'Suit yourself,' it says, 'No skin off my nose.' And off it flies out of the open window, watched idly by the cat. Doreen shakes her head. 'Vermin,' she says, though it isn't clear if she means the cat, its fleas, or the whole of fairydom. 'Time for a gin and wormwood.'

Hide and Seek

John is hiding. He is behind a bit of hedge, clipped as a peacock on the edge of the grassy circle in the castle ruins. His parents and Sally, who thinks she is grown up, are looking at boring labels such as "West Tower 1270," and taking photographs and saying things like "do you see that arch, it almost looks Romanesque. Extraordinary!" Hide and seek is more fun, even on your own.

A hen with ruffles around its feet waddles round the hedge and chuckles. 'Go away,' John whispers. 'You'll give me away.' Off it goes. Time passes.

Then the light changes, and John feels cold of a sudden. It would be warmer in the sunlight. So he decides he has won the game because they haven't found him, and emerges onto the grassy circle. Except that the sun now looks like the moon, and the light is silver. And there's nobody about. Not a soul. Anywhere.

It's not a big castle. He looks into what was the Banqueting Hall 1340, inside the West Tower 1270, even in the scary East Tower, with its sullen dark puddles of water at the bottom. There is nobody.

He runs to the gates. They are locked. He runs back to the grassy circle, he turns frantically round three times, seeing no-one, and bursts into tears.

When he looks up again, there is a figure in front of him. Silver grey, very tall, thin, shining in the moonlight as though wearing a body suit of foil. It is beckoning. John knows the dangers of talking to strangers. He looks round. There is another such figure behind him. And another. Three. He is in the middle.

Then there are lights outside the gates. Someone gets out of a car, unlocks the gates, and it is a policeman, and he and a policewoman come through, in uniform, no mistaking, and John runs to them because his mother tells him the police are safe and to trust them unless you are a very bad person, which he knows he isn't, and the policeman and policewoman speak comfortable words to him and tell him not to worry, and sit him down on a bench and give him a coke and some chocolate.

John sees that the tall silver beings are slowly circling around on the grass. The policeman sits on his left, the policewoman on his right. They pay no attention to the circling figures. The moon is high above. John feels serene.

The police stand up after a while. They stand and calmly take off their uniforms. They take them off, and underneath they are smooth and silver, as if wrapped in foil. Tall, thin, silver-grey, shining in the moonlight.

They take John by the hand and move over to the circling figures. John knows it is all right because they are police. They all join hands and circle round, smoothly, lightly. They move gradually faster. John sees that the figures and police have wings unfurling, gossamer thin so he can't quite see where they finish and the moonlit, star-flecked sky begins. They move their wings in lazy sweeping waves, they circle increasingly rapidly, and as one, slowly, drowsily, they all spiral up, up towards the moon.

And from a distance, John hears a voice, a voice he knows. 'John,' it says, 'come out, dear, and do stop being tiresome. It's time to go home.' It is his mother's voice. She sounds irritated with him, as usual.

John looks down, and there in the grass circle, in the sunlight, are his mother and father and Sally. Other people are wandering about, looking at the Keep, 1210, and the boring towers, and photographing them and themselves, or just standing chatting, or sitting eating sandwiches. John feels inclined to join his parents and go home.

He looks at the circles of figures spinning around him. They smile, so calmly, so warmly, despite the cold moonlight – smiles that speak of adventure and excitement and chocolate. His mother never allows him chocolate.

And John knows he must make a rather big decision.

Poohsticks

We were playing poohsticks. Dirk's boomerang-shaped stick sailed through in fine style. We leant over the parapet to see where my stubby entry would emerge. I had specially chosen it as least likely to get caught up in whatever there was below the bridge. We waited and waited.

'Bored,' said Dirk. 'Going home.' And off he stomped. I carried on watching, seeing how the eddies swirled. Sometimes bits of the river even seemed to go backwards. Then something appeared from under the central span of the bridge. It was small and green, looking for all the world like a pea-pod. There was something in it – a speck of thistledown perhaps. The pea-pod caught in one of the mini-whirlpools and turned lazily round and round, drifting nearer and nearer the bank.

I climbed over the fence and went down to the bank by the bridge. There it was, circling, caught, going nowhere. I thought I heard a faint cry, and realised that whatever was in the pod was alive. It was easy to steer it to the bank with a stick. I fished it out, and my heart sank.

How was I going to live this down? Must I keep quiet about it for ever? It is not good news for a 10-year old boy to find a fairy. It's bad for the image. However, Dirk had gone, and the fairy was talking. I had to hold it close to my ear to hear what it was saying. It seemed pretty angry. After a while it dawned on me that it wasn't speaking English. It was probably some ancient Gaelic tongue, I expect. It kept pointing to its leg, which was at a funny angle and on which was a small red patch.

What do you do with a fairy with a broken leg? I took it home, trying to walk very smoothly, because it kept whacking me with a minute paddle every time I jolted it.

My grandfather, with whom I live since my parents ran away, likes to think he's Irish, so he was delighted.

'Why, 'tis the best of luck to have a fairy in the house,' he said, as he used a matchstick to splint the creature's leg. 'You wait and see, my lad.' It was certainly lucky for the fairy, for grandpa devoted himself to it, softly crooning lullabies while the fairy stuck its fingers in its ears. I could resume my usual aimless 10-year old existence, interspersed with going to school. I said not a word to Dirk or any of the others.

What do you know of fairies? Not a lot, probably. Nor me. What sex are they, for a start? Was this 'little chap', as my grandpa called him, a boy or a girl? Whatever the answer, as soon as its leg was mended and it was able to get about again, it was clearly either female and gave birth extraordinarily quickly or it had some way of communicating with other fairies in the locality, for in a few days, there were some dozen in the house. Grandpa was beside himself with glee. 'For look you, lad,' he said to me, 'they don't take up much room, they don't require feeding, being as how they subsist on the nectar of sweet-smelling flowers, and they bring untold luck. And as for you, my boy, since you saved the little chap's life, you will be blessed for ever.'

He kept banging on about luck. I didn't altogether agree, as I lay in bed at night unable to sleep. They might otherwise be ideal house-guests, but they certainly knew how to party. They did it most of the night, most nights. I don't think grandpa could hear them, since their noise was very high-pitched and he was pretty ancient, but my young ears certainly could. They might have called it singing and high spirits, but I thought it about as attractive as caterwauling cats, and much more piercing.

Furthermore, the numbers were increasing daily. Even Grandpa was becoming a little irritated, but he'd started learning Gaelic and hoped in due course to be able to talk to them and encourage more reasonable behaviour.

And then one day, early November, I came back from school and the house was silent. They'd all vanished.

Grandpa was sitting in the parlour with something in his hands.

'Well, my boy. They've migrated. Why 'tis obvious when you think about it. Not enough nectar here in winter. They left this.' He handed me a small package wrapped in leaves.

I opened it. Inside was an acorn cup full of yellow powder. 'Gold!' I cried.

'No such luck, boyo,' said my Grandpa. 'It's foxglove pollen. Fairy Gold. They snort it, like cocaine. Ah well, it's all water under the bridge. Maybe they'll be back next spring.'

If they are, I'm running away too, like mum and dad.

Lime House

Come with me up this lane, my friend. What I want you to see is up there, some way beyond this terrace of cottages. When I was a kid it always felt like trespassing going up there, but at the same time irresistible.

The Lime House. That's where we're headed. Spooky.

All I knew, we knew, for sure back then, was that she was a witch. Miss Hagnose, that's what we called her. I'm sure it wasn't her name. A real witch. The kind that turns milk sour, people into toads, and gives your cattle boils. My mate Jerry said he'd seen it with own eyes so he knew it was true. I said he couldn't very well see it with anybody else's eyes and so he hit me.

'Don't doubt these things,' he said as he sat on my chest. I could smell his foul breath. 'Don't doubt it or evil will befall you.'

He frightened me. I was a bit of a pathetic specimen in those days. Miss Hagnose frightened me. The Lime House frightened me.

And then Jerry said I was a weedy squit who wet his bed and I had to do a dare to prove I wasn't. 'Promise,' he said, 'or I'll twist your ears.'

Because I was a weedy coward and hated getting hurt, I promised straight away. Jerry's ear-twisting was a terrible thing, believe me.

'You know,' he said, standing up and towering over me, 'you know why it's called the Lime House? Course you don't,' he went on, not giving me a chance to reply, ''cos you're an ignorant pig. It's called Lime House 'cos there's a lime pit in it.'

And with a terrible gleam in his eyes, he went on to tell me a lime pit was like a bath where you put people you've killed and it dissolves them right up, bones and all.

He let that sink in. Miss Hagnose disposing of people in her basement.

'She's a mass murderer,' he said. 'Not a lot of folk know that. All those people goes missing, that's her. All in the lime pit. Dissolved. Hair and teeth and clothes and all.'

'What missing people?' I asked him. I hadn't heard of any, only Grandma Davies' cat and he was so ancient he probably had just crawled away and died of oldness in the shrubbery.

'Don't you read the newspapers?' said Jerry.

I didn't, not then. Only the Beano. If Dennis the Menace had gone missing, his dog Gnasher would have tracked him down in a jiffy.

Anyway, there I was saddled with a dare. It hung over me like a terrible curse. The dare was, Jerry explained, that I had to get into the Lime House and collect a sample from the lime pit to prove I'd done it.

Despite my terror, I saw an obstacle. 'What in?' I asked Jerry. 'If it dissolves everything, how do I collect it?'

'A film cannister,' he said. 'Aluminium. Lime pits don't affect aluminium. Everybody knows that.'

So that was the dare. All I had to do was find a time when Miss Hagnose was out, find a way into the Lime House, find this lime pit, find a film canister, fill it up without getting any on me, get out again, and get away without being seen. What could go wrong, other than being dissolved or being caught and turned into a toad? Did I say that Miss Hagnose had this dreadful wart on her chin which sprouted hairs like a lavatory brush? She was a real witch.

Right, my friend. Here it is. The Lime House. A bit tumbled down now. Surprising the roof hasn't fallen in. Seemed bigger when I was a kid.

See what's in front of it? No, not the For Sale sign. That thing there pushing its way up into the sky? That, my friend, is a tree. A lime tree. That was why it was called the Lime House. No lime pits. Jerry's little joke to scare me.

And the dare? Oh, we'd forgotten about it the next day and decided to go fishing instead.

Donald and the Zligs

'I'm not going round there. They're Zligs!' Little Donald was adamant. He wasn't going there. His mother had told him to pop next door and ask if they had a cup of sugar to spare because she had run out. His job was to do as he was told. She had enough on her plate what with this and that and the other.

'They come from the planet Prodor,' said Donald. His mother said it was non-negotiable.

'They've got three eyes,' said Donald. His mother said he was going to have a sore bottom if he didn't stop being stupid and go at once.

To reach next door, you had to go out of the front door to the end of the path, turn right for a few yards, in through next door's gate, down their path and there was the door. Easy-peasy. But when you knew the door would be opened by a Zlig with three eyes, it was like the march to the scaffold and twice as long.

Donald dawdled. How his mother didn't know they were Zligs was a mystery to him. Grown-ups seem to walk around with their eyes closed. They saw what they wanted to see, and that was mostly things he'd done wrong, like his hands were dirty, or he'd torn his trousers. But he had talked to one of the Zligs when they first moved in. That was how he knew that they came from Prodor. As for their names, they were completely unpronounceable, so they called themselves unmemorable, ordinary things like John and Bill and Tracey and Mary.

It was Bill who opened the door. Or it might have been Tracey. Donald was fixated by the third eye. It seemed to float. A boy at school had once shown him how to hold two fingers up and squint, so that you saw double images, and you could make the two inner ones meet and then suddenly it looked like you had a third finger floating in the air between them. The third eye was like that. It made him feel sick.

'My mum says have you got some sugar to spare she's run out,' he gabbled.

Bill or Tracey asked what sugar was. He or she didn't ask out loud, but Donald knew that was what was meant. He said it was for making things sweet. That seemed to make sense, and the Zlig went inside and reappeared a few moments later with a small plastic box containing some powder. Donald assumed the box was plastic, but you never knew and it might be some super-modern, alien material. Whatever, it did the same job. Of keeping the powder inside and keeping the powder dry.

That, it turned out when he got home, was the main thing. Keeping it dry. As soon as his mother tipped a little of the powder into her cake mix, there was a fizzing, and the powder rehydrated into a remarkable assortment of sweets. Barley-sugars, lemon sherbets, toffees, humbugs, gobstoppers, after-dinner mints, jelly beans all popped into existence in alarming quantities. They spilled from the bowl onto the floor.

As it happened, Donald's father chose that moment to stagger in from his self-imposed vigil in front of the television. He was probably on the hunt for another bottle of beer, Donald thought. However, on seeing the bowl of cake mix overflowing with assorted confectionery, he began an inquisition.

Where had they come from? He looked dubious. How much powder was left? Most of it. How much did the current rehydrated selection weigh? What was the price in the shops?

Donald could see the way his mind was working. He wanted to set up a small but lucrative sweet business, and then likely take the proceeds down the betting shop.

The questioning continued. Could they extract some more powder from next door? He looked directly at Donald as he said this. After all Donald was on good terms with them.

'No, I'm not,' said Donald, and was ignored. After a bit of pacing round the kitchen table, Donald's father came to the conclusion that further negotiation for the powder fell to him. It needed his irresistible powers of persuasion, he said. In Donald's experience this usually consisted of shouting and going red in the face, but anything that didn't include him was just fine.

It was about a minute after Donald's father went out of the front door that the shouting began. It continued as he re-entered the house, as he stormed around the table, not only red, but with smoke coming out of his ears. It had gone, he bellowed.

Donald sneaked out of the door. It had gone. The house next door had vanished. Only a little smoke rose up from the neatly levelled ground.

In the middle was a small object. Donald went over and picked the object up. It was a small doll. It had three eyes. The middle one winked at Donald. In that moment, he decided that he would not tell his parents. There might be some money in this yet, but he would deal with it himself.

Castle Marigold

Marigold had a dream in which she inherited a castle from a distant uncle. When she woke, she found a letter on the mat from a solicitor telling her it was precisely so. 'Nice,' she thought.

She phoned in sick to work and set off to look at her inheritance. It was not far, along a side road she'd never noticed before, and by nine-thirty she had parked on a grassy patch in front of it.

It was bijou. A kind of two up, two down version of a castle. But castle it was. For a start there was a moat, full of water-lilies and a couple of ducks fighting their way through. There was a bridge over the moat, and a portcullis in front of studded oak doors. Her side of the bridge was a letterbox on a wobbly post, with a battered hunting horn dangling from it. Castle Walter was written on the side of the letterbox. That was her uncle's name. Walter, not the Castle bit. Marigold decided it would be renamed Castle Marigold, not out of conceit, but because...

Oh, all right, out of conceit, because she wanted to show off to her friends. Lizzie in particular. She would be green with envy. And the others in the shop where she worked. Drop in for coffee, she'd say. Any time. Just give a blast on the hunting horn and I'll raise the portcullis.

For the moment, the portcullis and massive studded doors seemed a bit of a problem. But as she walked over the bridge, as if by magic, and with splendid clanking-chain noises, the portcullis slid up, and behind, the oak doors creaked apart. And there she was, in a tiny courtyard, confronted by an ancient, wizened little man, who greeted her deferentially.

'Good morning, Miss Marigold,' he said in tremulous tones. 'I'm afraid I come with the castle. Please call me Trembling. Should you desire, you can dispense with my services, for I am somewhat past retirement age. But if you wish, I will stay. My terms are very reasonable, and I do know where things are.'

'Good to meet you, Trembling,' said Marigold. 'Please stay for now, and we'll see how things rock and roll.'

So stay he did. Marigold moved in without delay, and finding substantial sums of money were included in the legacy, threw in her job at Marks and Spencer.

The living accommodation was not extensive. Two bedrooms, living room, petite banqueting hall, gardrobe and kitchen. She looked forward to holding dinner parties in the hall, though probably with a max of six people, if they were going to be able to breathe.

Where Trembling's quarters were, she never discovered. He was simply there when she needed him, always courteous and obliging. Yet she found him creepy, so after a few weeks, she... well, to put it bluntly, she sacked him. 'Thank you, Trembling,' she said. 'I can manage perfectly well by myself, so perhaps it is time for you to take that well-deserved retirement.'

She gave him a generous parting gift to speed him on his way, and never saw him again.

Lizzie was coming round to lunch, all laid out in the banqueting hall. The sun was shining, and Marigold sat on a deckchair in the tiny courtyard at noon when the rays reached down into the castle. She sipped her prosecco and proclaimed 'Mine, mine. All mine. What a lucky girl I am.'

From without, the feeble farts of someone trying to sound the hunting horn sneaked in. Lizzie was here. Marigold languidly rose to let her in.

It was then she realised she didn't know how to open the great oak doors. Nor how to raise the portcullis. Trembling had presumably done these things in the past, for they had opened and raised when she approached. But from where he did this, and how, she didn't know. She searched every nook and cranny. Lizzie got fed up, texted 'Eff you, Marigold, you stuck-up bitch,' and went off to MacDonald's for something unhealthy.

Marigold spent the rest of the day searching fruitlessly. The next morning, in desperation, she phoned the police. 'I'm stuck in my house' – she didn't like to say castle – 'and I can't get out.' They told her to stop wasting their time.

There was no immediate need to leave. There were plenty of supplies. But in time everything runs out. Castle Marigold might be bijou, but it was built to withstand marauding hordes. Marigold stood on the little battlements, from which she could have poured boiling ylang-ylang oil on would-be invaders, and she yelled and she waved and she wailed.

A neighbour nearby fetched a long ladder and did the damsel in distress bit. Back on the civilised side of the moat, Marigold looked at her castle, and realised to get in and out in future she would have to use the ladder every time. 'Sod it,' she thought, turned her back on the castle for ever, and went to ask for her job back in M&S.

Are you safe at home?

Crackers

Their first Christmas. Kirstie has bought a Gressingham duck, which even now is overcooking in the oven. They gaze into each other's eyes and pull their crackers. Kirstie picks up the little present from her cracker, while Malcolm tries to untangle his paper hat.

'What?' cries Kirstie. 'What's this?' She holds up a snotty nose key-ring. 'Where did you get these crackers?'

'The joke shop,' says Malcolm. 'They're supposed to be funny.'

'I don't call snot funny. It's childish. It's what young boys snigger over.' Kirstie is fraught. The cooking has proved more complicated than she thought, and is currently going badly wrong, though she's not aware of it yet.

Malcolm looks around for the present in his cracker, which eventually he finds on the floor. It is a small, brown, wizened object reminiscent of something unpleasant, but with a tag attached to it, which has the two words "Pull me" on it. He pulls the tag. There is a sound as of a cosmic sigh, and the object begins to inflate, more and more. He has to back away from the table to make room.

It grows ever larger, tall, thin, dark. Four foot, five foot, six foot, seven foot high, and the creases pop out and it takes real shape. It is hard to believe.

'Hi!' says the inflated figure. 'The sprouts are burning.'

Kirstie screams and rushes over to the stove and takes the lid off. The dreadful aroma fills the air.

Malcolm manages to form words. "You're a genie!" he says.

"Bang on, young man," says the genie. "And I'm here to grant you three wishes."

"The sprouts..." cries Kirstie, a picture of distress.

'No probs,' says the genie, and with barely an Abracadabra, the sprouts are bright green, just cooked with a little bite left, glistening with butter. The pan is cleaner than when new. 'I've taken care of the duck too,' he says. 'It was significantly overdone. I like my duck a little pink.'

Kirstie says 'Oh,' and blushes. 'It's my first time,' she says. And adds, 'cooking a Christmas dinner,' just in case the genie thinks something else.

'Well, well, well!' says Malcolm. 'What a stroke of luck! Does every box of crackers have a genie in it?'

The genie looks him up and down. 'No,' he says. 'I replaced a fake dog-turd. Thought it might inject a little something into somebody's festivities. Now, what about another wish. Do you want a fortune?'

The couple look at each other and simultaneously say 'Of course!' After all, who wouldn't?

The genie concentrates for a moment and then says 'You're going to meet a tall, dark stranger. Other than me, that is.' There is silence. 'What's the matter? Not the sort of fortune you wanted to hear? Sorry! I'm afraid I'm a bit new at this game myself.'

He closes his eyes for another couple of seconds and mutters. Then he hands something to Malcolm.

Malcolm looks at the lump the genie has given him. 'What is it?' he asks.

'It's an uncut diamond of fantastic value,' the genie says. 'Should keep you in clover for the rest of your life. If you like clover, that is. Now your third wish?'

'Before that,' says Kirstie, 'I need to know, are you staying to dinner? Because if you are, I need to lay another place and Malcolm, you need to get the chair from the bedroom.'

'Would you like me to?' asks the genie.

She looks at Malcolm. He nods. 'Yes, we would, it's the least we can do!' There is a pause. Then Kirstie says 'Oh shit! That was our last wish, wasn't it?'

'Never mind,' says the genie, sitting on the elegant chair that mysteriously materialises at the table. "You've got that diamond, and a particularly fine meal to look forward to, thanks to me. Have you any wine?'

'Only one bottle,' says Malcolm. 'We can't afford...'

'Oh splendid,' says the genie. 'Fetch me a jug of water, would you.' Kirstie fills up a jug and places it in front of him. It turns deep crimson in a flash. 'I'm famous for it,' the genie says. 'Turning water into wine. You see...' He stands again, seemingly even taller this time. 'My little joke is that I'm not really a genie. I am just having a go in my lunch break. Rather like you lot play charades. My real name is Zagam.'

Kirstie and Malcolm look blank. 'Clearly not famous enough,' the stranger goes on. 'Go and Google me. Go on.'

Malcolm goes out to the bedroom, where the laptop is. Kirstie starts putting the food into dishes. The genie whistles quietly and changes the wine from red to white to rosé in a dizzying kaleidoscope.

Malcolm is standing in the doorway. 'I found him,' he says to Kirstie. 'Zagam's a demon of deceit and counterfeiting who has the talent of being able to turn water into wine.'

'There you are, you see,' says Zagam. 'I'm a demon. And you've invited me to supper.' He rubs his hands in a ghastly, lascivious motion. 'And I'm really very hungry. Not just for duck. But for souls. Happy Christmas!'

Product Recall

The alarm wakes me. I beat it into submission and doze off again. When next I surface, I see daylight sneaking in round the curtains, so I leap conscience-stricken from my bed and fling them wide.

My garden is not there. It's totally gone.

In its place, there is another garden, quite different. On either side, my neighbours' gardens are just as they were yesterday. In what was mine, where my little pond and rockery and rather mossy scrap of lawn lay, is a rigorous display of gravel topped with a small area of decking and an array of meticulous pots. And in it, leaning on the fence conversing with Trevor Atkins, my neighbour to the left, is a man.

Trevor spots me at the window, waves cheerfully, and carries on chatting.

In a trice, dressing-gowned and slippered, I am out there. My footsteps crunch on the gravel and the man turns. He smiles benignly at me. What do I say? I wave a hand feebly at the garden. 'Where...' I bleat, 'what...?'

The man looks at the gravelled and potted area and says, 'Oh, your wee plot. Product recall, my friend. Product recall. Some safety issue or other. Manufacturers called that model in. Asked me to fill the space temporary-like. Nature abhors a vacuum, you know. Can't happen.'

'But, but...,' I splutter. 'What do you mean, manufacturers? It's my garden. I didn't buy it. I made it. I dug the flaming pond. I hefted the blasted rockery stones. I planted them up.'

'He did, you know,' chips in Trevor from over the fence. Good chap, Trevor. Staunch ally.

The stranger is unmoved. 'You didn't buy it?' he says. 'Then seems to me the manufacturers bear no responsibility. They are not obliged to replace it with an updated model. They've done you a favour, saving you from an unsafe product. Let it be a lesson, my friend. You should always keep receipts, original packaging, that sort of thing.'

'But...' I begin, but nobody's listening.

'Try Citizens' Advice,' says Trevor. It's all very well for him to dish out suggestions. He's still got his garden.

'Look,' I say, 'these people, these manufacturers, whoever they are, what have they done with my garden?'

The man shrugs. 'Probably shredded it. I don't know the procedure exactly. More to the point, what about me? If you didn't buy the garden, the manufacturers aren't going to honour my expenses claim for all this.' It's his turn to wave at the gravel patch. 'Not to mention my wages. It's piecework for me, you know. Seems to me, it's your responsibility now to see me all right.'

This is outrageous. I've never heard its like. 'Don't be ridiculous,' I say to him. 'Take your garden away this instant.'

He shakes his head. 'Can't be done, my friend. I explained about nature and vacuums and that. Besides which, do you know how difficult it is to remove gravel? Now, about reimbursing me...'

At this point, Trevor saves me, for I am on the point of murder. Dressing-gowns have cords, remember, and cords can strangle.

Trevor addresses the man. 'Look mate, I'd quit while you can, if I were you. My chum here has a black belt at karate and a short temper.' He indicates me. The man looks terrified. Either he's a terrible coward or very gullible. Either way, off he runs.

'Thanks, Trevor,' I say. 'But what am I to do about all this gravel and stuff?'

'No probs,' he says. 'I have my army.'

He whistles and up his garden comes a procession of gnomes with spades and wheelbarrows. I've always regarded them as examples of bad taste, but clearly they have their uses. They troop through a loose paling in the fence and before you can say Rumplestiltskin, the gravel is on its way. To where, I have no idea, but go it does. Gnomes live in a different world.

'Do you want the decking left?' asks Trevor.

'Better had,' I say, for as the gravel goes, there is nothing there in its place. A sea of nothingness. We watch as the pots of plants gradually sink into invisibility, as into a bottomless bog. The decking will at least leave a bit of solid footing.

Trevor waves a hand at the black hole as it were. 'It'll be handy,' he says. 'You can chuck your waste out there.' He's right. It'll be a lot easier than the council's current complex system of boxes and bags and collection days and even and odd weeks.

As if to demonstrate its practicality, at that moment, Santa Claws appears on the fence to the right of what was my garden. Santa is right-hand neighbour's coal-black cat, who pays regular visits to our gardens to dig and desecrate and terrorise frogs in our ponds.

Santa leaps gaily off without properly considering where he is going. Trevor and I watch transfixed as he descends. He seems to float down for ever, like thistledown settling, his senses gradually realising that there is nothing beneath him, that he is heading for the slough of oblivion. His expression is of total flummoxment. His body, preceding his head, slowly dissolves into nothingness, and then his head follows, and the look of bewilderment remains like the Cheshire Cat's smile until last, until the tips of his whiskers and ears vanish for ever.

Good riddance, I think, and go inside to get some clothes on and have a belated breakfast.

Tea and Cake

When I opened the shed door to get my bike out, there he was, standing there as though he'd just knocked on the door to be let in, except that he was inside already. He was an odd chap. He would stand out in a crowd anywhere, except that he couldn't stand out, being only about three foot tall in his booted feet. But the king-sized beard and the shamrock green jacket and battered top hat were rather noticeable.

'Well and haven't I come a-visiting my long-lost kinsman, Seamus,' he said in a rich, brown brogue.

'Have you?' I asked. 'My name's not Seamus.'

'Listen to yourself now,' he said. 'And isn't the first-born of every O'Brien called Seamus, and aren't you the first-born of your father, bless his soul?'

'No,' I said, 'I have six older sisters.'

He dismissed them with a wave, and stomped out into the garden. 'Yer father wouldn't be going about christening them Seamus, now would he?'

'And,' I continued, following him as he moved among the raised veg beds, 'I am not Mr O'Brien, I am Mr O full-stop Brien; surname Brien, first name Oswald, initial O. Mr O. Brien.'

'All smoke and flimflam,' he cried, squashing a cabbage white caterpillar on a cabbage leaf. 'I know an O'Brien if I see one. Your daddy's mammy's daddy must have tried to make out he was English, that's the long and the short of it.' He extended an arm towards me. 'Will you not shake the hand of your second cousin four times removed's niece?'

I must have looked a little confused, because he immediately added, 'Nephew, I mean. Not niece, nephew. Or thereabouts.' He stroked his luxuriant beard reassuringly and pointed to the abundant growth of my Charlotte crop which were just beginning to flower. 'Potatoes,' he informed me. 'Would you be knowing that potatoes were invented in Ireland by one of the O'Briens in the time when Brian Boru was High King. Oh, glorious times those were! Would you be offering me a cup of tea and slice of barm brack or perhaps porter cake to help it down by any chance?'

I protested that I was just come to fetch my bike to go to the library, because I had a book overdue.

'Sure, and it can wait,' he barked. 'What book can it be that you are in such a hurry to get rid of it?'

'As it happens,' I said, producing the book in question from my backpack, 'it is WB Yeats' Fairy and Folk Tales of the Irish Peasantry. It's due back today.'

He looked up from his scrutiny of a runner bean and snorted. ''Tis a travesty, that book, a scourge, a blight. There is only one mention of a leprechaun, and that merely in passing. It is a mortal insult and I recommend you return it to the library as swiftly as humanly possible and shake your fist at them. I hope you did not pay good money for it. But first that cup of tea you promised. Sure and you don't expect me only to eat runner beans, raw and stringy, with my having a delicate stomach as it is, for all they too were invented in Ireland.' He lumbered off towards the house, and what could I do but follow him? But I did object to his allegations that my beans were stringy.

***

Much later, when the bottle of Jamieson's was completely empty... now there's a funny thing. I've always preferred Irish whiskey – not as a child, obviously, when vile concoctions like Dandelion and Burdock or Lucosade were my preferred tipple – so maybe there was truth in the little chap's assertion that in the dim past, my family had tried to suppress evidence of an Irish ancestry. Maybe that was why I'd picked out that WB Yeats volume on the library shelves, because I had no conscious interest in either folklore, nor things Irish, as I thought. I mentioned all this to the little chap, and he said it was a common thing, to be in denial about Irish roots, and a monstrous disgrace, because the Irish were denied credit for so many great inventions and discoveries. The light bulb, Kentucky fried chicken, Buddhism, to name but three, he said, which many folk would be wholly gobsmacked to learn originated in the Emerald Isle.

Anyway, much later when the Jamieson's, which had been a new bottle, I may add, was all gone, I must have nodded off, because the next thing I knew it was morning and I was still in my armchair in front of the gas fire which was merrily blazing away.

And the little man was nowhere to be seen. Nor was my prized collection of receipts for every cup of coffee I have ever bought. That hurt. It could mean nothing to anybody else, but to me it is a collection of little caffeine moments that form footsteps through my life.

And the WB Yeats had gone too. A few days later I saw it in the Recently Returned rack in the library. I picked it up and opened it, and a slip of green paper floated out. On it, I read, "Thanks for the tea. One day, I'll be back for the cake." Maybe the little chap had a shred of decency after all. I'll stock up on the Jamieson's just in case.

Trapp

At 7.45, Matthew is woken by the Thing. It sits on his bedside table and vibrates and flashes and screams until he picks it up.

'This is your lucky day!' the screen proclaims, while a cartoon demon hops up and down blowing up balloons and releasing them with blood-curdling screeches. 'Touch me for a glimpse of tomorrow,' the screen reads.

Matthew gingerly extends a forefinger and presses the Thing. His daughter gave it to him the day before, 'to drag him into the modern age of networking,' she said. It was a Phablet, she explained. A sort of cross between a smartphone and a tablet – awkwardly large for one and inconveniently small for the other, particularly with elderly eyes.

Now it seems the Thing has a life of its own. It announces that he's been selected from millions to road-test the beta version of a new app called Trapp – the Truth App, it boldly asserts. In pulsating letters, it commands: 'Say "I am honoured." Say it out loud!'

Hardly awake, Matthew says, 'All right, then. "I am honoured." Will that do?'

Across the screen scrolls 'All right, then. "I am honoured." Will that do?' And underneath, in a box labelled The Truth, appears "What an infernal cheek! I need a pee!" Both of which statements are indeed passing through Matthew's mind.

The cartoon demon capers across the screen. 'There you are!' it says in an oddly accented voice. 'Trapp listens, and tells you what a person really thinks!'

Beneath it is the statement: "Note: this is a development version for testing and not fully functional. We will request feedback in seven days." The demon wags a finger at the statement, and declares, 'Free for a week!

Use and enjoy!' In the Truth box, Matthew reads, "Ooh, don't I so envy you!!!" With three exclamation marks.

It is at that moment that the radio alarm switches itself on. Matthew instantly recognises the inquisitorial tones of one of the regular presenters of the Today programme.

'People might say, might they not, that you are avoiding the issue, the *very real* issue of...' and so on, he is saying. A transcript of the words scrolls across the Thing's screen as the presenter says them. Beneath, the Truth box reads, "I want a cup of coffee."

His victim, whose voice Matthew doesn't recognise, starts replying, clearly saying nothing in a circumlocutory fashion. The truth box reads, "The presenter chappie looks like a wizened prune. I want a cup of coffee."

The interview soon ends, giving way to the weather forecast and the news at eight. According to the Truth box, both the weatherman and the news reader are pre-eminently yearning for a cup of coffee too.

This, thinks Matthew, is less than world-shattering. Over breakfast, however, he does discover that there is a setting he can alter in the Trapp app, affecting the depth of truth that it uncovers. At maximum, it reveals embarrassing fears and neuroses and prejudices that, frankly, should only be aired on a psychiatrist's couch. Matthew does not want to know. At the other end of the scale, it seems to reveal such banal things as the desire for a cup of coffee. Maybe, Matthew thinks, but does not say aloud, it has some interesting possibilities after all.

So he takes it with him on his daily constitutional in the park *en route* for his favourite coffee house. Birds sing, dogs bark. He looks at the Thing. Trapp declares, "In the beta version, functionality is limited to human speech."

Well, well! So in the final version there is a hint of a possibility of understanding what the birds and animals are talking about! Except that Matthew thinks it will probably turn out to be things like "Get off my patch!" or

"I'm hungry!" or "Can I sniff your bottom?" Some things are better not understood.

In the café, he orders a latte and a brownie, and is relieved to see that the Truth box says he really means he wants a latte and a brownie, nothing else. The girl behind the counter says, 'No problem,' while the Truth box tells him she means it is a real nuisance because she was in the middle of telling Stacey about last night.

By the time Matthew is nearly home, he is fed up with discovering that most people seem to be self-centred and self-engrossed, and politeness is a sham. A neighbour down the road's apparently cheery "Morning, Matt. Lovely day!' transpires to hide a message of "Go away, you boring old sod."

But as he turns into his front garden, a youth on a bicycle mounts the pavement at speed and before Matthew can take in what is happening, has wrested the Thing from his hand and sped off down the road with it.

Matthew has a peaceful afternoon, evening, and night. He phones his daughter, and with a clear conscience, tells her that the Thing has been stolen. He can go back to being a happy Luddite, innocent of what others think of him. It is bliss.

And then in the morning, there on the front doorstep is the Thing. And a note.

"Sory I took it. They all thinks Im evil. That Trapp showed me the error of me ways."

Matthew heart sinks. It seems he is trapped by Trapp. But then it occurs to him that nobody but he and the criminal know of the Thing's return, so he takes it to the canal and drops it in, where it sinks like a stone. Alas, to his horror, the cartoon demon rises from the waters like a phoenix from the fire, and circles round until Matthew is giddy, and settles on his shoulder and whispers in his ear, 'Thank you for freeing me, mate! Now I'll be with you always to tell you what folk really think of you! Fun, fun, fun, fun!'

Celandine

She was young, she was beautiful, and she came out of the cold-water tap. Percy covered his modesty with the sponge.

'Excuse me,' she said. 'My name is Celandine, and I'm here to make a formal protest.'

Percy was affronted. 'No,' he spluttered, 'I do not excuse you. It is an unwarranted liberty when I am defenceless and in an embarrassing state.'

'Don't blame me,' said Celandine, 'if you let yourself go to pot. If you had a torso like Sean Connery you would be proud to expose yourself, but the neglect and overindulgence of years...'

'I'm reaching for the loofah,' cried Percy, 'and I'm warning you...'

'Pooey,' she said. 'Loofah's are nothing to me.' She wafted a hand in the air and the loofah deliquesced into a semi-viscous fluid, which dribbled onto Percy's mountainous stomach.

'That's not fair,' he expostulated.

'Not fair? Not fair?' Celandine exploded in return. 'Do you call it fair when a debased, renegade, earth elemental crashes head-first into your home? Is that just? Is it right?'

'What the hell are you talking about, woman?' said Percy. He reckoned she was a woman, or at least womanish. It was hard to focus precisely on her, as she seemed to waver and wamble when he looked at her. She was possibly naked, or enveloped in some wafting gauzery.

'Nibbles,' she said.

That at least rang a bell. Nibbles was Percy's garden gnome. 'Ah, Nibbles,' he said. 'Little chap, pointy hat, stout...' he looked down at himself, '...stoutish, beard, lives down on the rockery.'

'Correction,' snorted Celandine, oscillating wildly, 'lives upside-down in my home. My cosy, bijou residence wherein I have been quietly minding my own business for aeons. Remove him, sir.'

Percy was outraged, and almost let the sponge slip. 'Why? I didn't put him there. Wherever there is,' he added.

'My habitation,' she said in pompous tones. 'I believe you call it your garden pond. *Your*, you note. Not *the*. Did you dig it?'

'Don't be idiotic. I don't go around digging ponds. It's a pathetic apology for one anyway...'

'Bijou,' corrected Celandine.

'...covered in duckweed...'

'Insulation, that is,' she said. 'Like you have a duvet.'

'I don't,' he protested. 'I've only got the sponge. But you miss the point, miss. I didn't put Nibbles there, if indeed there he is, so why in tarnation should I remove him, eh? And get my hands wet into the bargain?' As he said that, he realised it was a pretty feeble excuse for somebody wallowing in a bath.

'You did it by proxy,' she said, and wilfully flicked cold water at his face.

'Blast your eyes,' said Percy. 'Riddles again.'

'Your dog pushed him in. *Your* dog,' she clarified.

'Shambles.'

'It is,' she concurred. 'My house is now, as well.'

'No,' said Percy, 'my dog's name is Shambles.'

'He's a disgrace,' Celandine pronounced. 'You should keep him under control. I want Nibbles out. I want compensation. I want assurances that it will never happen again.'

'Go to blazes,' said Percy. 'Get back up that tap and flow away. What are you, anyway?'

'I'm Celandine,' she said. 'Why don't you listen?'

'What, I said, not who. I don't care what your blasted name is.'

She sighed in an aqueous way. 'I am an Undine, ignoramus. Like Nibbles is a Gnome, Shambles is a mangy mongrel, and you're a sort of human.'

'Sort of? Sort of?' he snorted. 'Anyway, what's an Undine?'

'I'm a Water elemental. Like Gnomes are Earth elementals. Nibbles should be down in the soil, digging away or whatever, not strutting about on the surface and falling into people's homes.'

'He's liberated,' Percy said. 'Anyway, I'll see if I can fish him out. As for compensation, as I said, go to blazes.'

He rose from the bath.

'Oh cripes!' said Celandine as his excellence displayed itself before her eyes, and fled back up the tap.

The Cold Caller

The woman at the door, she's tiny, she's ancient, her hands are gnarled. Above the shabby green coat, a purple felt hat wears a drooping peacock feather. She holds out a scraggy bunch of heather. 'Lucky heather, ducky?'

Digby turns into the house and yells, 'Do we want any lucky heather, dear?'

Faintly a reply of 'No,' floats down the stairs.

'No, thank you,' says Digby to the old woman.

'Have you heard the Good News, young man?' she asks.

'Have we heard the good news,' shouts Digby.

The voice from upstairs goes on a bit. Digby seems to understand. He turns back to the woman and interprets it. 'It seems we have, and it isn't as good as it's cracked up to be.'

The old woman appears to be about to argue, but changes tack and asks him, 'Have you been involved in an accident recently, dearie?' She sniffs and wipes her nose with the back of her hand.

After the call and response up the stairs, Digby says, 'It seems we suffered a blister on our hand through over-zealous use of the trowel while gardening.'

'Both of you?' asks the old woman.

'Both of us?' Digby is perplexed.

'Never mind that, ducks,' says the old woman. 'How about you sue the trowel for assault and battery?' Digby's puzzlement is manifest. A nearby wood pigeon tells them his toe hurts, Betty. The old woman tells it her toes hurt too and her name ain't Betty. 'Look ducks,' she says to Digby, 'it would save time and me feet and me temper if you told me what exactly you do want, instead of all this guessing.'

'Is there anything we want?' yells Digby up the stairs.

The disembodied voice is clear. 'We need some eggs.'

The old woman says as it happens she has half-a-dozen on her person, and produces an egg box from her copious layers of clothing.

'Are they free-range?' comes the voice from above.

'Are they free-range?' repeats Digby unnecessarily.

The old woman opens the box and squints at the eggs. 'Five of them are,' she says.

'And the sixth?'

'It ain't free-range,' the old woman clarifies.

'I see,' says Digby. After a brief exchange with the voice, he asks her how much they are.

The old woman thinks. 'I'd settle for a cup of tea and a slice of cake and a sit down,' she says.

The voice aloft says no. So Digby offers a pound, which the old lady grudgingly accepts and wanders off down the street, coughing.

In the kitchen, Digby opens the box and looks to see if it obvious which one is not free-range. One after the other they talk to him:

'The egg next to me is the one.'

'The egg diagonally opposite is free-range.'

'The free range egg is in the corner of the box.'

And so on. Unfortunately, it is not possible to tell which egg's voice is which, so no amount of logic will tell what the answer to the conundrum is. On the other hand, one egg does look a bit odd, though Digby can't say in what way. He picks it out to examine it closely, and drops it. It is probably carelessness, or perhaps he is startled by something, but it seems to him the egg wants to be dropped. When it hits the floor, it breaks.

He expects gloop to seep over the floor, but instead a little, dense cloud of fog exudes outwards. As it clears, he sees a small figure there, green with a purple top and a minute limp peacock feather on top of that. The figure grows alarmingly quickly. Before he knows what is happening, it speaks:

'I'll be having that cup of tea now, young man. And if you can run to a piece of cake...'

Digby considers he has no choice. While the old woman sits creakingly down, he puts the kettle on and find himself apologising for only having some biscuits. She eats three of them grudgingly, and suddenly points a gnarled finger at him.

''Ere young man, you're a whatsit. a will-o'-the-wisp, that's what it is. You know, dearie, one of them what throws his voice.'

'A ventriloquist,' sighs Digby. He's not often caught out.

'That voice upstairs...' she says.

Digby waves a deprecating hand. 'I live alone. Me and the cat.'

'What cat's that, my lovely?' the old woman says, a simpering grimace on her cracked lips.

'He ran away.'

She struggles to her feet. 'Nice cup of tea,' she says, 'shame about the cake. Have a lucky sprig of heather anyway, ducks.'

At the front door, he watches her shamble away. When she is out of sight, he closes the door and starts upstairs. As he climbs, his hair recedes and turns white. By the time he reaches the top, his steps are shaky. He holds on to the bannister here, leans on a door frame there, and shuffles through the bedroom door. Slowly, achingly he lays himself down on the bed beside the figure already there. It is incongruously dressed in a shabby green coat and a mauve hat with a limp feather in it.

'Sleep now,' she says, but her lips do not move.

He clutches the lucky heather and drifts off.

Broken Wing

Late on Friday night, Florence Pithy left the Nag's Head and hobbled back to the dark alley round the corner from Boots where the entrance to her flat was.

As she fumbled about trying to locate her key, she became aware of a presence on the doorstep. Perhaps a bundle of clothes. Or a hay-bale, or a stuffed St Bernard dog.

It spoke. 'Hullo,' it said. 'Can you help me? Oh, the indignity.'

Florence found the key. 'Got it,' she cried. 'Tally-ho and up we go.'

'That's the trouble,' said the heap. 'We don't. We can't.'

'No such word as can't,' said Flo. 'Shift your carcase.'

And somehow the two ascended to the heights above Boots, the one bumping off the walls as usual after the Nag's Head, the other complaining that he had never used his stair-climbing muscles before.

'What?' said Flo. 'I know them stairs is a pestilence. What do you do instead? Fly?'

'Yes,' he said. 'But I've broken my wing. The left one.'

Flo wiped the drizzle off her glasses with a finger and saw he had indeed a pair of five-foot high wings, one of which, the left, drooped sadly.

'Tut tut,' she said.

'It's these high cranes on construction sites,' he said. 'I failed to notice the jib of one against the dazzle of the setting sun and, crack, I was flying around in circles.'

'Tut tut,' repeated Flo. 'What was you doing up there? You a drone or what?'

'On my way to a client. Routine visit.' He looked desolate. There was a certain radiance about him but the drizzle had taken the edge off, leaving only misery. 'What am I to do? I'm supposed to do the supporting and helping, not this way round.'

Florence removed her bedraggled hat and squinted closely at him. 'You're a flipping angel, or I'm a banana,' she said.

He sighed. 'Yes. A guardian angel. Can you help me?'

She sniffed. 'Have a sit down and a bite to eat and drink. 'Scept you angels don't need no physical food, I am given to understand, being as how you have no corporeal bodies.' She looked dubiously at his physique, which on better days, must have been exceedingly impressive. 'Or do you eat manna? I'm fresh out of manna.'

'No, we don't,' said the angel. 'We don't need to eat. But I do anyway. It might cheer me up. Thank you.'

Flo meandered into the kitchen while the angel gingerly arranged himself on the sofa, left wing propped along the back.

In a brace of jiffies she was back with two half-full tumblers and two slices of chocolate cake.

'Oh, come on,' said the angel. 'Devil's Food Cake. That's not funny.'

'It is not,' she snapped. 'It's me granny's special Pick-you-up Cake. It's 40% proof. And the tipple, Mr Angel – what's your name, eh?'

'Gabriel,' he said.

'What. *The* Gabriel. The archangel chappie?'

'No, no. There are lots of Gabriels in the angelic host. It's a common family name. My first name is Nelson.'

'Oh yeah, and your dad was Walter, I s'pose,' she cackled obscenely.

'How did you know?'

'The tipple,' Flo said, ignoring him, 'is of my own devising. I call it Bitters. A bit of this, bit of that... It'll put hairs on your chest.'

'But will it mend wings?' The angel took a swig and a couple of minutes later was able to breathe again.

Flo meditatively chewed cake. At last, 'a splint,' she cried. 'I've got some toothpicks somewhere.'

'I think you're thinking of mending fairies' legs,' said Gabriel.

Flo gazed at the wing. 'S'pose. Need something bigger. Splint. Splint. Ah, I know...'

She left the room. In a moment, she returned brandishing... 'a broomstick,' she cried, and offered it up to the broken wing. 'Too long. Shame I don't have no saw...'

'That's not a problem, said Gabriel, and from somewhere produced a flaming sword with which he chopped a foot off the broomstick.

And so it was, with the aid of a couple of crêpe bandages as found in every good citizen's First Aid box, his broken wing was splinted. He flapped it carefully in the confines of the room. It seemed to work.

'Thank you,' he said. 'Now if you don't mind opening the window...,' and out he flew.

Florence watched him go. 'I wonder what'll happen now,' she mused. 'Maybe I should have told him I was a witch, and not a nice one at that. That stick has form, it has. It is wasn't for me piles, I'd be using it still.'

Once upon a time...

The Sparrow and the Glove

Long ago, there lived a Sparrow, who was lonely. He went to visit the Town Cat, who went everywhere and knew everything.

'I am lonely,' he said, 'now that my family and friends have all disappeared. How do I find a mate?'

'I am not a sparrow,' said the Cat, 'how should I know, even though I go everywhere and know everything?'

'If I had a mate,' the Sparrow went on, 'we could produce lots of baby sparrows and the world would be full of noise and laughter once more.'

'So you could,' said the Cat, and smiled at the thought. 'Well, my friend, first you must fall in love.'

So the sparrow flew here and there, and high and low, looking for love, but all the robins and ducks and three-toed snipe, and even the majestic swans left him cold. Sadly, he was returning to his lonely home when he spotted something red on the ground. He flew down and picked up the daintiest, thistledown-soft glove you can imagine, the colour of ripe cherries.

'Someone has lost this,' he thought. 'I will ask Town Cat if she knows who, because she goes everywhere and knows everything.'

The Town Cat thought hard. 'I think it belongs to the Princess Passerdena,' she said, 'but I can't be sure it is her I see walking through the town, because the Princess always wears a veil. She is so beautiful, they say, that anyone seeing her face would immediately fall hopelessly in love with her. She only removes her veil in the privacy of her bedchamber, and even I, the Town Cat, cannot venture there.'

'Thank you,' said the Sparrow, and at nightfall, with the glove in his beak, flew up to the window at the top of the high tower where the Princess' bedchamber was. Through the window, he saw the veiled Princess enter the room, and tapped on the glass. Princess Passerdena opened the window, and there she saw her red glove in the Sparrow's beak.

'My glove!' she exclaimed. 'How can I reward you, little sparrow? Will you take this ring?' And she slipped a ring off her slender finger and slid it onto his leg. Then she closed the window, and that was that.

Except that the Sparrow didn't fly away. He hid round the corner where he could spy in without being seen. He saw the Princess prepare for bed, and eventually she took off her veil.

The Sparrow stared. Her lips were the colour of cherries, her eyes the colour of ripe acorns, and her hair of golden sunlight. The Sparrow fell off the window ledge, hopelessly in love, and remembered how to fly just in time.

He went to the Town Cat.

'I am in love with the Princess,' he said, 'but I am only a lowly sparrow, not a Prince. What shall I do?'

'Let me think,' said the Cat, and twisted herself around in circles seven times. 'I know,' she said. ' We will wait until the Princess is out walking, then you pretend to be injured and I will pick you up in my mouth. When the Princess sees her ring, she'll know it is you, and then what will happen will happen.'

So the next day, the Cat carried the limp body of the Sparrow in front of the Princess.

'Oh goodness,' she cried. 'That is my ring! What have you done, you cruel animal? Drop my friend the Sparrow this instant or I shall stamp my foot.'

So the Princess Passerdena knelt and picked up the little body. She carried it tenderly to the Castle and up the stairs to her bedchamber. The little Sparrow's heart was beating so fast, he was sure she must know he was only pretending to be injured. But she said, 'You poor thing! There is hardly any life in you. I will kiss you and that will make you better.'

So she lifted her veil, and bent down, and with her cherry-red lips, kissed the little form, and the moment her lips touched the Sparrow, there was a blinding flash.

A little later, there came flying down from the high tower, not one, but two sparrows, twisting and turning in the golden sunlight and making such a noise. One had eyes the colour of acorns and a tiny cherry-red spot on the tip of her beak.

And they made their nest in the high branches of a tree, where the twigs are slender, because the Town Cat was too heavy to climb that far. And they all lived common or garden lives ever after.

The Three Ducks

Once upon a time there was a miller, who had a daughter called Rosabella. She caught a chill and nearly died, and ever after was pale and weak, so that she could no longer help her father in the mill.

'She must go,' said the Miller. 'I can't afford to keep her if she is no use to me.' So he gave her three small loaves of bread tied in a cloth and three pennies he had been saving up, and sent her packing.

Rosabella walked all day, and her steps became more and more feeble as first the sun beat down on her, and then the rain came and soaked her to the skin.

'Alas,' she cried, 'I shall die if I don't find some shelter soon!' and at the moment she spied an inn beside the road.

'Come in, come in,' said the innkeeper. 'You can have a room for the night for one penny, and a dish of mutton broth for another penny.'

Rosabella thought: 'If I spend two pennies here, I shall have only one penny to keep me for the rest of my life! I shall take the room, and eat one of my loaves of bread for supper.'

So she undid the cloth and found the loaves of bread were completely wet from the rain. 'I can't eat those,' she thought, ' I'll have to pay for a bowl of mutton broth and let tomorrow look after itself.'

The broth was the best she had ever tasted, and she went to bed better fed than ever she did in her father's mill, and slept like a baby.

In the morning, the innkeeper's wife secretly gave her a packet of bread and cheese sandwiches, because she was a sentimental woman and felt sorrow for Rosabella, who looked so thin and pale. Rosabella set out on the road again, feeling hopeful that something good would turn up.

After a while, it started raining again, and so she decided to shelter under a bridge and eat her sandwiches. As she opened her mouth to take a bite, a duck swam by and said 'Won't you give me some bread, pretty maiden, for I am so hungry from all this swimming?'

'Of course,' said Rosabella, 'I've got two more sandwiches, and that's more than enough for me,' and gave her the sandwich. The duck swallowed it in one gulp, and quacked twice. Immediately another duck came swimming under the bridge. 'Give me bread,' she said, 'or I will die from hunger.'

And Rosabella remembered the kindness of the innkeeper's wife, and thought 'I'll still have a sandwich left for me. That is all I need.' And she threw the second sandwich to the second duck, who swallowed it in one gulp and quacked three times.

At that moment a drake came swimming under the bridge. 'I, too, am in dire need of food,' he said. 'If you give me your last sandwich, I promise you you will want for nothing for the rest of your life.'

The drake looked at Rosabella with great big brown eyes and her heart melted. 'I will feel awful if I don't help him,' she thought, 'and besides he has promised, and a promise is a promise, and besides, he has such honest brown eyes, and besides I still have one penny left, with which I can buy food for today if the worst happens. Tomorrow can look after itself.' and she threw the sandwich to the drake, who gobbled it in one gulp.

Rosabella held her breath. 'Surely something must happen now,' she thought. 'Surely he'll lead me to a good man who will love me and look after me for ever and ever. Or perhaps he will turn my one penny into gold and jewels.' She felt a little silly thinking that way about the humble penny, but even so, she took it out to see if it still looked the same. At that moment, the drake quacked very loudly and startled her, so that the penny fell from her fingers into the river and she watched it gurgle its way right down to the bottom. A shiver of horror went down her spine and she felt her heart stopped.

Then beside her there was a cough, and she looked up, tears in her eyes. There stood a man in a suit with a big brown rosette in his lapel. 'Thank you for your belief in me,' he said. She noticed the drake had vanished.

'Are you,' she stammered, 'are you a prince?'

'No, bless you, dear girl. I am a politician, and your belief in me has released me from the drake form into which I was turned by the party whip. Now I can continue my passionate commitment to make the country a better place so we can all live happily ever afterwards.'

And off he strode without a backward glance.

Going to the Dogs

The traveller descends from an ancient bus into an ancient village square. As he knew there would be, there is an inn there, which is to be his base.

In the morning, following directions given by the innkeeper, he trudges on forest tracks to visit Herr and Frau Beckmesser. After a while, he meets a small boy with wild hair, who looks at him with wide eyes.

'Hallo,' says the traveller, 'you are Wolfram?'

'Yes,' says the boy. He must be about seven years old. 'You have come to see Mutti and Hansi.'

'I have,' the traveller replies, 'but mostly I've come to see you.' The boy continues to look at him, a steady, unnerving gaze. But the traveller is used to such things. He speaks gently. 'Take me first to your...' He stops. 'Your grandparents?' he suggests.

'I call them Mutti and Hansi,' says the boy. 'They told me to. Follow me.'

And off they go along the track. Lightly, the traveller says, 'You were with the wolves in these woods before you came to live here?'

'With the dogs,' corrects the boy. 'Are you from a newspaper? Hansi said to me...'

'Do you remember anything before the dogs?' interrupts the traveller.

Wolfram leaps ahead and points. 'We are here,' he announces. They have reached a little clearing, with a little log cabin. And there in the little garden, a little old man, more whiskers than face, is digging.

Thus begins the first of several days that the traveller spends talking with the Beckmessers, or rather, listening to Mutti, who is unstoppable. The boy says little. Sometimes he is there, sometimes not.

In the evenings, over beer and goulash at the inn, the traveller reflects. He has learned very little he did not know already from the papers a few years ago, in the flurry of interest when the boy first emerged from the forest and was taken in by the Beckmessers. How he had no language, and preferred to eat from a plate on the floor, growling if anyone came near.

Mutti endlessly tells him anecdotes about how quickly the boy has acquired language since then, and picked up human behaviour, but there are no real new clues as to the boy's history. Only one thing really interests the traveller. He learns that most days, Wolfram goes off on his own into the forest for an hour or two. When Mutti asks him where he goes, all he says is 'I am going to the dogs.' They cannot stop him.

The traveller decides he must discover where the boy goes. The next day at the cabin, while listening to Mutti, he notices Wolfram slip out of the room. He apologises to Mutti, and follows discretely. The boy walks into the forest with great purpose, looking only ahead. The traveller soon sees he has no need to be too secretive, so he walks quite openly, just keeping the boy in sight.

But as they penetrate deeper in among the dark pillars of pines, it seems to him that the little figure in front of him is changing. It is growing taller, and the head is changing shape, though he cannot tell how.

And soon he finds he has to jog to keep up. It seems the figure is skimming over the ground, not walking at all. He breaks into a run and races after, snap of twig underfoot and panting breath deadened by the forest. And then suddenly there is light ahead, and the figure, now more an incandescent globe, floats out into a clearing, bursts into dazzling light... and vanishes.

When he has his breath back, the traveller examines the ground. There is nothing out of the ordinary. Should he return to the cottage to see if the boy returns? He is not worried about becoming lost in the forest, for he is the traveller, and besides, the journey has taken no more than fifteen minutes.

And so he is drinking coffee with Mutti a couple of hours later, half listening to her tale of when Wolfram saw a cat in the village for the first time, when the boy comes through the door, and squats by the fire as if nothing has happened.

When Mutti pauses for breath, the traveller asks to have a word alone with Wolfram. He takes the boy outside. The traveller sits on a log, the boy crouches, fixes his unnerving eyes on him, and waits.

'I followed you into the forest this morning, Wolfram,' the traveller says. 'I think you know who I am.' He meets the boy's stare, and raises his eyebrows just perceptibly.

There is a man seated on a log outside a cabin in a clearing in a forest. A boy is crouched on the ground in front of him. The boy rises, moves towards the man, reaches out a hand, and touches him on the temple. The scene freezes for a moment. Then the man rises.

'I must be going,' says the traveller, but Wolfram takes his hand and leads him over to the cabin. 'Come and meet Mutti,' he says excitedly. 'She has many tales to tell about me, and she has coffee ready for you. Do you come from a newspaper? Hansi says I must beware of newspapermen, but you seem nice.'

'A newspaper?' says the traveller. 'I suppose I must do. I never knew that before.'

The two go inside the little cabin. In the little garden, a little old man, more whiskers than face, looks up from his digging and smiles.

The Clockmaker

Every year about this time the Clockmaker came to the town. The clock in the town hall tower was exceedingly elaborate. Each hour a door opened and a procession of strange figures processed round a semi-circular track and into a door the other side. There were arguments over what the figures meant. Some were obvious: a mother with a babe in arms, a child spinning a hoop, a young woman with a basket of corn on her hip, a gaunt hooded shape with a scythe. Others were part-human: a dwarf with one arm, pulling an outrageous face, a man with a raven's head exposing his bottom to the crowd, a tall elegant woman in a long gown from under which poked a pair of horse's hooves. Others were not of this world and had no names that anyone knew. Sometimes you might think you recognised them from your dreams and nightmares.

But that was not all. At midday, after the procession, doors above the clock opened and an amazing astronomical scene was revealed. Planets and comets moved in complex orbits round a sun. As the last stroke of twelve struck, the most extraordinary thing happened. An eclipse. Darkness spread over the scene from the right until it was entirely dark, then it gradually revealed again as the darkness moved left. Nobody knew how this was done; it was high up the tower and difficult to see clearly. The general opinion was that it was simply magic. Betsy Forester did not think so. It was, she argued to her friend, Tom, the odd-job boy who had no surname and a strange tic, unlikely, since the Clockmaker came each year to look after the clock and he didn't look like a magician or sorcerer or wizard or anything like that. He didn't have a long nose and a cloak for a start, just a pair of spectacles and a bald pate. He was more like your favourite grandfather.

'I don't have no grandfather,' said Tom.

'That don't make no difference,' said Betsy. 'You can pretend.'

'It does though. Means I can't win the Clocky.'

'How do you work that out, Tom?' said Betsy. 'It's got nothing to do with it. It's all how you behaves.'

'Yes, but if you have no family, who's to tell the Clockmaker you've been good?'

'Other folk. I'll tell him.'

'He won't take no notice of you.'

'You wait. I'll wiggle my bottom at him.'

'You wouldn't dare! Would you?'

'Wait and see!' cried Betsy, pinched Tom's backside and dashed off. He chased after, but she could always outrun him.

The Clocky was a coveted prize. Each year when he came to service the clock, the Clockmaker brought a mechanical toy with him. This was the Clocky. It might be a duck or a cat or even man-like. And it did things. You wound it up and it acted. The duck flapped its wings, waddled a few steps and quacked, very life-like. The cat stretched, arching its back, then suddenly its ears went back and it hissed and everyone screamed.

Each year a new toy. Each year the Clockmaker gave it to the child who had behaved best during the year since his last visit. Never did a town have so many polite children. How the Clockmaker chose was a mystery, but he talked with the important folk of the town, including the schoolteacher and the priest, so maybe they told him. Since the children had no idea how he decided, they played safe and behaved impeccably, even at home. Well, mostly.

There was, however, one important person in the town whom the Clockmaker never consulted. Overshadowing the town was the castle, wherein lived Duke Von. Visitors and newcomers to the town tended to suggest that he must be Von Something, but he wasn't. Just Von. He was a large man with flesh like blancmange. He and his mother, the Dowager Duchess, lived in the castle alone, if you can call living with a small army of servants and cooks and butlers and gardeners and equerries being alone. For years the Duchess Von had tormented the castle, the town and the surrounding district appallingly. Count Von was her pet, spoiled and cosseted. Now that the Duchess was almost entirely bed-bound, the Count, aged forty or so, had a new-found freedom.

The Clockmaker could arrive any day. To say the town was agog would be overstating it, but there was something in the air. He always lodged at the Cocked Snook, where Betsy's father was the the innkeeper. Betsy's mum tended the bar and allowed no drunkenness, singing or impropriety. Her father was the inn's memorable cook. During the Clockmaker's stay, an almost shrine-like aura hung over the inn. The Cocked Snook kept the Clockmaker's room available from May Day so they would not be taken by surprise, but he'd been known to arrive as late as the Night of the Five Frowns.

Tom was earning a few pence cleaning the gullies at the castle. Being ill-fed and small, he was nearly invisible, so as he shovelled away in a particularly gruesome gully, he was most surprised when a nasal tenor cried out 'You, boy!' He jumped. Nobody addressed him at the castle except the Clerk of the Outer Parts, who paid him a couple of groats or a farthing for his work every now and then. He turned to see Duke Von glaring down at him truculently. That he was the Duke was clearly indicated by two lines of lackeys and flunkeys forming an arrow-head with the Duke at the point. Tom had not seen the Duke in the flesh before. And of flesh there was plenty, veiled in splendid but ludicrous garb to be sure, but evident.

'You are a child,' stated the Duke. His retinue nodded and mumbled murmurs of appreciation at this insight. Tom wiped his brow with the back of a filthy hand.

'Don't tug your forelock at me, boy,' cried the Duke. 'I don't like... don't like...' He faded into silence. His vocabulary was not large, thanks to preferring self-indulgence to study.

'Obsequious behaviour, my Lord?' said the flunkey on his right, who was his Personal Admirer, or PA for short.

'Don't interrupt me!'

The PA cringed. The Duke turned again to Tom. 'Are you good, boy?'

Good at what? Tom looked around, hoping to see the answer in the gully or on the walls.

'You are to win the Clocky for me,' said the Duke. 'From the Clockmaker.'

'How can...?' Tom cried out, then stopped. He thought it probably wasn't a good idea to question the Duke, but it just slipped out.

'Don't bother me with questions, boy. Toady, deal with it.' And off he stumped, the train of lackeys fluttering after him like a skein of geese flying off into the sunset. Only the PA remained, the unfortunate whom the Duke called Toady. His real name was Edward, which over the months the Duke had shortened to Ted, then lengthened to Teddy and finally migrated to Toady. It was fitting but it rankled.

It didn't take Toady long to find that Tom knew nothing of how the Clockmaker made his decision. And as for winning...

'Me win? More likely that wall would fall on your head, Sir.'

Toady looked at the wall. It had been built to withstand besieging hordes and looked likely to remain that way until the crack of doom. The barometer of his future career at the castle pointed to dismal.

'You seem to be polite and well-behaved,' said Toady, managing to sound wretched and supercilious at the same time. 'If not you, who?'

'Someone else.'

'I can work that out, stupid boy.' He changed his tone to smarmy. 'I'm sure you have your ear to the ground.'

'What d'you mean?'

'You know what's what...'

'What what's what?' The man talked rubbish, as most did at the castle. Like some sort of code.

'I'm sure there's nothing much happens in the town that escapes your notice. Young man,' he added ingratiatingly.

'Me, I don't know nothing.' said Tom. 'D'you mean who I think'll win the Clocky? Could be anyone. Could be Betsy, like as not. If she don't wiggle her bottom.'

'Who's Betsy?'

'Friend.'

'You have a friend?'

'Sort of. Anyway, she's clever and she's good. And she's all right.' Tom sniffed noisily.

'I see,' said Edward 'Toady' Firkin-Blank. 'I see...'

Betsy was not feeling very good at that moment. She'd just eaten a large piece of squab pie in the Cocked Snook's larder after meaning to sneak only a sliver. It was a sad coincidence that as she emerged and started running retching towards the privy, she collided with a man just entering the courtyard. The dust from his journeying was removed from his boots in an unconventional manner.

When she had finished, Betsy wiped her mouth and looked up into those eyes, and those eyes looked back at her over their spectacles. "I think maybe you've just learned something," they seemed to say. Betsy rushed for a bucket of water and with the hem of her dress, washed the man's boots. He stood still, blinking like an owl.

'And what is for supper, dear girl?' he asked.

'You must ask me dad, sir,' said the wretched thing. The innkeeper was approaching, hand outstretched.

'Welcome, Mister Clockmaker, sir.' For indeed it was he. 'Room's ready. Come and have something to eat after your journey. I've a good joint of beef, pig's cheek, braised lampreys, or a fine squab pie. Betsy, take his bags up, there's a good girl.'

The Clockmaker glanced at Betsy, his feet, and the bucket, and said, 'The beef sounds excellent, Landlord. And I can manage my own bags, thank you.'

Betsy went off to the stable and cried into the straw for a bit. There it was later that Tom found her.

'Clockmaker's here,' she sniffled.

'I got to find who's going to win the Clocky,' Tom said. 'They want to know up the castle. Toady give me a groat. Then I'll get a farthing if I tells them right. How much is that together, Betsy?'

Betsy burst into tears again, and sobbed something.

'What's that?'

She pulled herself together. 'It's a farthing and a groat.'

'Don't it have a name?'

'No.' She glared at him.

'Duke wants the Clocky. I reckon he'll force whoever wins it to give it over. If you wins it, Betsy, I won't tell them. Never!'

'I'll not win. I sicked on Clockmaker's boots.'

They stared stubbornly at each other until, inevitably, one of them started giggling.

The next evening, as Betsy walked home from the school, a lean hand sneaked out from a dark alley and dragged her in. She found herself looking into Toady's lugubrious eyes.

'You, girl,' he said in a hoarse whisper that squeaked, 'if you win the Clockmaker's prize, you are to give it to the Duke.'

Betsy was not the least intimidated by the skeletal stranger. She recognised him from Tom's description. 'You're Mr Toady, aren't you?'

'Don't call me that!'

'The Duke does.'

Oh, why were children so perverse? Toady could charm venom-tongued Dowager Duchesses into purring kittens, but children... He fought for dignity and found a vestige in a long-forgotten corner of his being.

'If you do not give the prize to me, girl, your friend,' he almost sneezed the words, 'Tom, your friend, will lose the little employment currently afforded him by the Duke's...' What was the word? '...behest,' he finished. It wasn't right, but even so Betsy's eyes widened, and he knew he'd found his target. He smiled inwardly. "Benevolence" – that was the word. He didn't need it now.

For the next four days, the Clockmaker worked his alchemical skills on the great clock, its mysterious figures, its extraordinary eclipse. Each evening, he ate the landlord's latest creation, now roebuck cutlets, now goose and pease pudding, now swaddled carp, probably poached from the monastery pond. Afterwards he gave audience to perplexed citizens and local worthies. On the fourth and final evening, however, he asked the landlord for Betsy to be sent up to him.

She went in with trepidation and emerged some minutes later with an astonished expression and a small bundle wrapped in cloth. Out in the courtyard, she stopped and froze, thinking... thinking... Then with a shake of her head, she slipped into the stables. Tom was there, as she expected. It was often his bed for the night.

'Take it,' she said. 'Take it to fatty Duke.'

'No.'

'You must.'

'I said if you was to win it I would never tell.'

'Tom, listen. Clockmaker says to do it. He knows, Tom, he knows everything. Take it to the Duke, Tom.'

'Have you looked at it, Betsy? What is it?'

'No, I haven't. It's not for me, he made it for the Duke. Oh!' She put her hand over her mouth. 'Clockmaker said I wasn't to tell nobody.'

'Well then, I ain't nobody. So you can tell me everything.'

'I can't, I can't, Tom. Do it, will you? For me. Don't be pig-headed.'

'Pig-head yourself. All right, I'll do it. But I wouldn't for nobody else!'

Tom ran all the way to the Castle, and entered it by ways only known to small wiry boys with devious minds. He headed towards the greatest noise, which came from the Great Hall. The Duke was making merry in a solitary and gluttonous manner, fêted by flunkeys. Tom walked straight up to the table and held up the package.

There was sudden silence. Duke Von looked at him. Those little eyes in the blancmange of a face became greedy gleaming gems. 'The Clocky,' he said, stretched out and grabbed the package. 'Clear the table,' he yelped, and minions fluttered to oblige.

Toady came into the hall at a loping stumble. 'I have just been told, my Lord. It is outrageous...'

'He has brought the Clocky.'

Toady stopped short. The Duke, tip of tongue extruded, unwrapped the package. Candle and firelight sparkled from a small object. From the shadows, Tom watched raptly. He could not identify what it was as the Duke wound a key, churning power into the clockwork. Done, Duke Von creased his corporation over the table and placed the Clocky as near the centre as his bulk allowed. And stood back.

It was a mouse. With a whirr, it turned towards the Duke and reared up on its back legs, little round stomach protruding, nose quivering, beady eyes fixed on the Duke's. Thus it stayed, that fraction longer than is comfortable. Such was the concentration of attention from Duke and retinue and Tom, that none seemed to breathe. The odd crack of logs in the fire marked the passing of time.

Then the Clocky uttered a tiny squeak and dropped to the table, turned and started running in circles, faster and faster. No, it wasn't circles, it was a spiral. It ran and ran, each circuit further out from the centre. It ran while the assembled heads swung back and forth following its progress, like pendulums in some human clock. Then the mouse fell off the edge. It exploded on the floor into a pool of cogs and springs and all was quiet.

The stillness of the Duke was terrible. The minions knew his moods, his tantrums. They waited fearful.

The Duke drew a long breath and rose to his full height. With a soft voice, deeper than his usual petulant shrilling, he said, 'I'll to bed now. It has been a tiring day and there is much to do tomorrow. Much to do.' The lake of lackeys broke like a wave as he passed through, then flowed after him in his wake.

Tom was left alone with Toady, who was examining what has been the Clocky.

'Do I get me farthing?' said Tom.

Toady looked up at him blankly for a long moment. Then he searched his robes, found a coin and held it out to Tom. 'Something has happened here today, boy,' he said. 'It would not do to talk of it. I can trust you.' He swirled away, a cadaverous question mark.

Tom crouched down by the remains, picked up a cog and fitted it into another piece. He remained there some hours into the small of the night, undisturbed. Whatever was happening in the Castle, it was happening elsewhere. At some point, he feasted on the remains of the Duke's banquet. It was an act of kindness to the unappreciated kitchen staff.

The next morning, Betsy took a slab of bread and some chitterlings to the stables, where she found Tom asleep in the straw. He woke at her touch, then wrinkled his nose.

'What's those?'

'They's chitterlings. My dad says they're right special. I stole them for you.'

'They look like innards. Like when you cut open a rabbit.'

'That's cos they are, stupid.'

'I don't want none of them. Anyhow, I'm full up. Eaten enough for a week, me.' He patted his little round stomach.

'How's that, Tom?'

'Never you mind. I'll tell you later. When you tells me what Clockmaker said to you.'

'Oh! I'd forgotten. Clockmaker wants to see you. You're to go up when clock strikes nine.'

'Me! What for? What have I done wrong?'

As the clockwork in the town hall tower spun into action triggering the clapper into hammering the hour bell nine times, Tom, a tad tidier than usual, knocked on the door of the Clockmaker's room. Betsy waited a long time on the stairs.

When the door opened again, the Clockmaker stood there with his hand on Tom's shoulder.

'I'm to be his prentice, Betsy,' said Tom. He looked up at the Clockmaker, who was not a tall man. 'He ain't got no children of his own, and he says I've got good hands.'

'And a remarkable aptitude,' said the Clockmaker. 'Show Betsy.'

From behind his back, Tom produced the Clocky. 'It fell off the table at the Castle and broke. I put it together again.'

'He did, but not quite as I made it. He changed it in certain ways. Remarkable. Even I do not know how it will perform now.'

'Here you are, Betsy, it's for you.' Tom looked mysterious.

Betsy took the clockwork mouse.

'Wind it up,' said Tom. 'See the key? Then put it on the floor.'

She turned and turned, placed the mouse on the floor and stood back. With a whirr, it swivelled towards Betsy and reared up on its back legs, little round stomach protruding, nose quivering, beady eyes fixed on hers. Suddenly the Clocky uttered a tiny squeak, dropped to the floor, and started running in circles, faster and faster. No, it wasn't circles, it was a spiral. It ran and ran, each circuit closer and closer to Betsy. Then it shot up her leg beneath her skirts.

Betsy screamed. The mouse fell to the floor and burst apart. Tom ran. Betsy chased after him, still screaming. The Clockmaker smiled benignly, and closed the door. He knew that Betsy was the faster runner. He knew everything.

The Shepherd and the Princess

Dickon was a shepherd lad. All summer he lived out on the hills with the sheep, sleeping under trees. Each week, Martha, daughter of the owner of the village store, brought provisions up to him, otherwise he saw nobody. Martha thought Dickon wonderful, though he was in truth an extremely dull boy. He knew sheep and was pretty accurate at weather prediction, but that was the extent of his learning. But Martha was a very simple girl herself, and considered their exchanges the height of sophisticated romantic discourse.

''Ere you are, Dickon,' she would say when she managed to find him, under a sycamore like as not, chewing idly on a twig.

'Ta,' he would say, and take the basket.

'Till next week then.'

'Aye.'

And back she would trudge, her little heart aflutter. Hopelessly.

At night, sleeping under the stars on the mossy sheep-trimmed sward, or snuggled in a thicket so close knit that raindrops left it well alone, Dickon dreamed of a Princess. She had amber eyes, golden hair and teeth like pearls, and what happened in those dreams we cannot know, but it left him dreamy-eyed and woolly-headed, appropriately for a shepherd boy.

One day, he spied three people on the hill coming towards him. At a distance, Dickon thought them hunchbacks and possibly aliens from a spaceship, for the previous evening he had seen a strange bright light streaking through the sky. But as they neared the fallen tree trunk on which he sat, he saw that they had packs upon their backs, sturdy boots on their feet, and stout sticks in their hands.

'Morning, fellow,' one cried. 'Fine day for a good blow.'

'Ugg,' said Dickon.

'Tell us, young yeoman, are we on route for Castle Arcadia, wherein dwells King Grizzle of the Wayward Eyebrows and his fabled daughter, Princess Ambrosia?'

'You what?' said Dickon, who had never heard of it or them.

'You must know of her at least, worthy rustic, of her amber eyes, honey hair and pearlescent teeth.' The three men laughed easily, confidently.

'Castle?' said Dickon.

'So 'tis said, good fellow. So we are assured by the landlord of the Three Cocks. 'Tother side of yonder ridge, he said. Ripe for the plundering.'

The other two gentlemen concurred.

'King Grizzle is a curmudgeonly soul, 'tis said, and wont to set challenges and quests for those seeking the hand of his daughter. But we three have brains and brawn and base cunning, have we not, boys?'

'Spoken truly, d'Arcy, for are we not scholars and gentlemen,' said one of the others.

'And sportsmen,' added the third.

The first, d'Arcy, led a brief cheer to celebrate their genius, and then turned to Dickon. 'Pray tell us, fine fellow, the best path over yon ridge.'

Dickon considered. 'Dunno,' he said. 'Sheep don't go there.'

d'Arcy snorted. 'Then we must trust to our wit. Say, what do you know of the King and the angelic Ambrosia, fellow?'

Dickon reckoned that Ambrosia must be the princess of his dreams according to their description, but what he knew of her from those encounters was not for the telling. 'Nothing,' he said. 'Never heard of no King, nor no Castle neither.'

'Fellow's a half-wit,' scholar number two said. 'Let us go, and leave him to his wool-gathering.'

Dickon watched them toil up the slopes until they were out of sight. Thoughts wandered around his simple mind. He was no scholar, no gentleman, no sportsman. What chance could he have with a bad-tempered King and his demands? But Dickon was practical, in a sheep-tending and keeping himself reasonably dry in the face of unseasonable weather sort of way. Simple souls look for simple solutions, that was his philosophy, if he knew what that word meant.

So it was, that when Martha arrived with his supplies on the morrow, she found herself being appraised by a practical eye. 'Yur, Marth,' Dickon said. 'What say...' He trailed off, suddenly embarrassed.

Martha blushed beetroot. 'Don' mind if I do,' she said.

'You're a right princess, you are, Marth,' said Dickon.

'Well...' replied Martha, and doffed her bonnet and shawl with alacrity.

The Woodcutter and the Princess

There lived in the mountains a wood gatherer named Stefan. He said he was a woodcutter, but he did more gathering than cutting. When the winters came, as reindeer can sniff out green blades of grass beneath the snow, so Stefan could sense dead wood and dig it out.

Thus it was, one day in December, that he shovelled away at a drift and uncovered a wooden post which turned out to be the top of a magnificent throne of gilded splendour. And in the throne, a princess, white and delicate, but frozen solid and hard as stone.

Stefan dragged the throne and Princess to his hut on his sledge, and stowed it in his woodshed. His housekeeper, Gretl, declared that the Princess should be left there to begin defrosting slowly. It would not do to bring her in to the fire, she said, for a swift thaw would cause immense pain as the blood began once more to course through the Princess' veins, and would be insufferable to a sensitive creature such as she, with her translucent alabaster skin. And she, Gretl, knew about such things, for did she not hibernate in winter before she became Stefan's housekeeper? For Gretl was a red squirrel and had beaten off all competition for the job by virtue of having a built-in duster in the form of an enormous tail.

Over the weeks, as the Princess was gradually moved nearer the warm, Stefan resolved to go to the City to find if they knew of a missing Princess.

At the Tourist Information Bureau, they suggested he ask at the Lost Property Office. The girl there asked him what sort of princess it was. Stefan said she had golden hair and skin like milky parchment, and he could not describe the colour of her eyes for they were still frozen shut, but he was sure they would prove to be clear, lambent azure.

The girl pursed her lips. 'How do you know she is a princess?' she asked.

By the heavens, Stefan thought, these city-folk are dull bumpkins. He spelt out as to a child that she was sitting on a gilded throne, therefore she was a Princess.

The girl consulted the screen and said no princesses had been handed in on the buses, on the metro, or on the trains in the last five years.

After patiently explaining that he thought this was a Lost Property Office, not a Found Property Office, Stefan lost his temper and left in a huff.

In sore need of refreshment to pacify his enraged spirit, he happened upon an internet café hard by. He demanded a flagon of dark ale, and to know whether they had heard of a missing Princess.

After much misunderstanding, he had to be content with a cappuccino and a swift introduction to a computer on which he might Google missing Princesses. Alas the best the machine could produce was the Grand Duchess Anastasia Nikolaevna of Russia, who would be 114 years old now, and whom DNA evidence, whatever that was, had subsequently shown had actually been murdered along with Tsar Nicholas II, his wife and his other daughters, and was never missing at all.

Back in Stefan's hut, the Princess opened her eyes, which were chestnut brown. She prodded the alabaster skin on her forearm. She pressed down, she removed the finger. The flesh remained dented. 'Alas,' she cried, 'where is the natural elastic resilience of royal flesh in the prime of youth? What is beneath my translucent ivory skin? Is it butter or clay? Ah, woe is me. It is too much to bear.'

At that moment, a red squirrel bearing a carved wooden cup from which steam was rising entered the room and approached the throne. Had Gretl been able to understand courtly Croatian, and had studied cryogenics at university, she might have been able to explain that a certain loss of skin tone was to be expected after freezing and thawing. But she couldn't and she hadn't.

The Princess, however, had been brought up to perceive squirrels as vermin. She screamed in an uncourtly manner and flung the cup to the ground. It was not an auspicious start to her rebirth.

By the time Stefan returned, deeply aggravated by his experiences in town, the Princess too was in a galactic-sized strop. It was beyond a joke. So luring her with tales of a fantastic palace up in the mountains, Stefan bundled the Princess up on the sledge and up the heights they went. At a remote place, he dumped her on the snow, and started yodelling. The appalling noise triggered a minor avalanche. It quickly returned the Princess to her prior permafrosted state. And they all lived happily ever after.

Some Day

The girl at the Information/Ciggy counter looked bored, sulky and about fifteen. It wasn't that she wasn't busy. The queue stretched nearly to the door, mostly seeking to smoke their lives away or gamble themselves into penury with lottery and scratch cards. No. She looked bored and sulky because she thought it cool. She looked about fifteen because she'd put in an hour's cosmetic enhancement before work. You never knew, after all.

And there, three back in the queue, was a Prince. Stacey – that's our girl – was simply a romantic. She knew some day her Prince would come. Actually he came several times a day, but turned out when he reached the counter to have bad teeth, or LOVE and HATE tattooed on his knuckles, or a Birmingham accent. Or he just wanted ciggies, not her. But she lived in hope.

She sent the first in the queue on her way clasping a book of second-class stamps. Only two to go. She was sure the Prince was trying not to be seen looking adoringly at her, and cultivated her most sullen expression to give him encouragement.

The next customer was a simple twenty Embassy request. But then he span it out by finding he hadn't enough cash even if he searched every pocket, and eventually used his Debit card, and then at the last minute decided he'd have a scratch card as well, and which one was the best? And Stacey said she didn't know, which was true, why should she, but he looked suspiciously at her and chose the one furthest away from her.

One customer to go, who plonked a ten-pound note on the counter and pointed to the cabinet behind Stacey while talking incessantly and loudly into her phone.

'Yeah she did, yeah, yeah, yeah, she said 'e'd 'it 'er so bad she 'ad to go to A an' E an' d'you know what Debs, she never pressed charges. She could of, Debs, it warn't the first time like. Yeah, yeah, I know, I prefer Corrie too. You remember that bloke...'

Stacey got twenty Marlboro, which were roughly in the direction the girl was pointing. The girl's hand waved violently from side to side and indicated to move to the right. So Stacey fetched twenty Benson and the girl snatched them up, opened the packet in one deft movement, phone clasped between shoulder and ear, and stuck one in her mouth, never pausing in her monologue. Then she walked off.

'Your change!' cried Stacey, but the girl was out of the door. Stacey shrugged, thought of pocketing the change, and then, meeting the steady gaze of her Prince, now standing tall – well, tallish – and handsome directly in front of her, only two feet in front her, decided taking the money might reflect badly on the character of a future princess and put it in the till. Her heart did a couple of cartwheels and she fluttered her eyes, hoping her eyelashes were on straight.

The Prince smiled weakly. 'Do you doh if you thtock gooth fat?' he asked, and sneezed violently. He had a lisp. 'I've got a code,' he continued unnecessarily. 'I want to rub it on by chetht.'

Stacey sighed. Another time, another place, talk of rubbing things on chethts might be rather exciting. But here and now she saw his eyes were watery and slightly bloodshot. She tried to feel she wanted to nurse him until he was better and could sweep her off to his palace, but she failed. So she pressed a button and bent to a microphone and said: 'Nevil to Info, Nevil to Info,' though it sounded nothing like it as it boomed around the store.

To the Prince she said nothing, because it wasn't cool to use words unnecessarily, and simply looked at the next customer and said "Yeah?"

The rejected Prince shuffled to one side, and shortly a spotty fat boy arrived and took him on a little guided tour of the supermarket, ending at the holy grail of goose fat.

The Prince was absurdly grateful, and it is to be reported that in a few days, his cold was gone.

Stacey went home at the end of her shift and consoled herself as usual with wine and chocolate. Tomorrow, more Princes would arrive, and some day...

Meanwhile, in town...

Taking off

I'm hidden behind a wheelie bin at the end of a cul-de-sac. Zac and the Bishop are at the open end of the alley, knowing I am in there somewhere. A bad, bad situation.

'If only I could fly,' I think, and look up as though I expect a life-saving rope to be dangling from a passing helicopter. Only bleak walls of bleak buildings punctuated by barred windows.

I can hear the Bishop whistling. Sounds like a hymn. That means he's pleased with himself, zeroing in for a kill. I know the procedure. The Bishop is the muscle, but lightning fast and relentless. He will be moving down the alley first, sniffing out hiding places, whistling. I recognise *Jesus wants me for a sunbeam*, and feel my stomach heave with fear. Farther back up the alley, Zac will be watching, eagle-eyed, spotting any slight movement in the gloom and mess. If I manage to break past the Bishop, Zac will have me. Which is better, I ask myself? It's no choice. The result will be the same. If I survive at all, I will probably wish I hadn't.

I close my eyes. 'If only I could fly,' I think again, and I wish it with all my being, more than I wished for a bicycle for my sixth birthday, more than I wished I would be picked for the school soccer team, more than I wished Elly would say yes when I asked her. None of these ever happened. Even so, I'm wishing now.

I feel desolate, that the bottom has dropped out of my world, no hope, no hope, and I am falling, falling, falling, bottomless. There is nothing underneath me. I open my eyes and gasp. I'm not falling; I'm floating. About a foot off the ground. I concentrate, and think 'Up.' And up I go by another foot. Careful now, or I will be visible over the wheelie bin. The whistling is sweatingly close. The Bishop has moved onto *All things bright and beautiful*, and is clicking his fingers along with it. I reckon I have a couple of minutes before I am revealed.

I screw my eyes shut and focus as never before. 'Up and fast,' I think, 'faster than...' And before I can decide how fast, I open my eyes and I have shot up through the air until I am floating well above the buildings round the alley. I can see their flat roofs. The alley is a dark gash below. I hold my breath to see if I can hear the Bishop whistle, but there is this rhythmic beating filling my ears. It occurs to me that without meaning to I am shrugging my shoulders in time to the beating, like some reflex action. It occurs to me that I can see something out of the corner of my eye. It occurs to me, as I twist my head round, that I have wings. Big! Feathery! Capable! It seems perfectly natural. I stop shrugging my shoulders and soar, gently tilting and twisting, awakening dormant instincts.

In my childhood, I often lay in bed before dropping off to sleep imagining what it would be like to fly. Oh, the adventures I could get up to in my dreams! Now, by some miracle, I can have those adventures in reality. And yet, I find there's only one thing I want; to get back at Zac and the Bishop. They have humiliated me so many times, sapping what little confidence I have, laughing when I fail the initiation tasks they set me. With astonishing expertise, I fly down into the alley. They stand gazing up at me, mouths open as if catching flies. I look at them standing there, small, puny; mere nothings. My anger evaporates. Instead, I simply feel pity. They are small shrivelled souls, to whom life had been terrible, and who, through their petty tyranny, are trying to feel like somebodies, somebodies who matter. Perhaps, I think, compassion flooding through me, I can help them find themselves, become somebody.

I land near them. For my first landing, it is impressive, I reckon. They think differently. They flee, scampering away as fast as they can, screaming like babies.

'Oh, sod them,' I say, and flap my wings. Taking off is a bit more difficult than landing. If you've ever seen swans and geese pedalling frantically along to achieve flight, you'll understand what I mean. But eventually, with effort, I am floating and then flying again, and the freedom is indescribable. The best feeling ever. Forget Zac, forget the Bishop, forget humiliation. I am king of the skies!

Then I hear laughter, and looking up I find I am not alone. I am being laughed at by another winged man floating above me. It is different from Zac's mocking though; this is good-humoured laughter.

'Hi there,' he says. 'That was pretty good for a first attempt! Forget those two; they're well beyond a bit of kindness. Come and have some fun. You deserve it, all you've been through. Let's see how well you fly.' And off he shoots, off towards the glorious sunset. And I soar after him, on top of the world. Where are we going? Who knows? Do I care? Somebody wants me for a sunbeam!

Breakfast Time

Carla's cafe at 8.00 am is usually funereally quiet, save for the hissing roar of the coffee machine at intervals. I like it like that. I gradually surface, the eyes softly learn to focus on the newspaper, the brain cranks itself up for rational thought. Carla knows what I want, so the coffee and toast appear without my asking. I'm a creature of habit.

Today, however, there is interference in the gentle nurturing stillness. A voice is singing, far far too cheerfully. *Summertime*, it warbles, *an' the livin' is easy.* I can hear the *g* missing from the end of *livin'*, true to the lyrics. The noise seems to be coming from the kitchen, which is in the back room, I assume. At least, that's where the toast appears from.

'Carla,' I state, 'someone is in your kitchen, singing.'

Carla sticks her head through the beaded curtain into the back room, and withdraws it again. 'Nope,' she says. 'It's just you and me, darling.'

'Can't you hear it?' I say, annoyed that at least for the moment the voice has stopped.

Carla is completely still for a few seconds. 'I can't hear nothing, darling,' she says. 'Not a dicky bird. Must be your imagination. Toast all right?'

'Yes,' I say, not having tasted the toast, which I usually take with half Marmite, half honey. Carla gets them in specially for me, so she says. 'It's stopped at the moment,' I add, 'so you wouldn't hear it.'

'Ah,' she says, and lets off a blast of steam from the coffee machine as if it were the Royal Scot just drawn into the platform.

At that moment, the voice strikes up again. I don't recognise it for a bit, until it gets to the line *Be like the kettle and sing*. It's the sort of line you don't forget. It worms its way into your head and festers there.

'There you are!' I cry.

Carla looks at me with an expression I once saw on my maths teacher when he peered over my shoulder during my disastrous O-level in the course of his invigilatory perambulations.

The voice begins to scream, very high, very loud. I place my hands over my ears. Carla is staring at me now. She says something, but I can't hear her, only the screaming. It seems it's only a foot away. Then something touches my leg. I push myself back from the table so fast that the chair catches and overturns.

When I come to, I'm sitting back at the table, only Carla is trying to make me drink something. I sip. It is tea, heavily sweetened, which is anathema to me. I try to protest, but she says 'Ssh, now. There, there, darling. It'll make you feel better.' It won't. It doesn't. My head hurts.

'Look, Carla,' I say, 'Will you stop it? I never drink tea. You know that. Have you gone completely barking? Where's my coffee?'

'You had a funny turn,' she says. 'You look a better colour now. Does your head hurt, my darling?'

'No,' I say, and pick up the coffee, which I observe has been sitting there all the time. 'And can't you turn that radio down?'

'What radio, my darling?' she says. 'I don't have no radio.' It must be the mystery voice, imitating Radio 2 this time.

The voice starts on *Twinkle, twinkle, little star*, so help me, and not in tune. It is the last straw. Maybe I should buy one of those i-player things. Stick Wagner's Ring on it; all sixteen hours. If I'm to start hearing voices, I'll choose whose voices they are.

I pay Carla and leave. A hundred yards down the road, the breeze through my little remaining hair makes me realise I've left my hat behind. I retrace my steps, to see though the door, Carla, her face purple, is hurling bread rolls at a corner of the room. Something is cornered there, fending them off with a fish-slice. It looks remarkably like – what? – a pixie. Forget my hat. Some sacrifices are worth making.

Tomorrow, tomorrow..., it's Caffé Nero, I think. Doesn't do to get set in one's ways.

Tunes from a Tin Whistle

He sat there in the middle of the underpass, silent. All we could hear, apart from the muffled roar of the traffic overhead, was the drip, drip from embryo stalactites dangling from the brick-arched roof. His presence was scary. We hesitated. Molly said 'Let's go the long way. I don't trust him,' and we all felt the same.

Yet we stayed there a moment and gazed along that tunnel, bleakly pooled with weak light at intervals. Gazed at that small dark figure cross-legged, as it seemed, sitting up against the wall under one of the lamps. We stayed transfixed. What held us, I can't say. It was, looking back, a scene from a real-life film noir. It seemed a beginning, not something to walk away from.

And then, he picked something up and put it to his lips, and the strangest tune wafted down the underpass, like a wisp of air. It was unlike anything I have ever heard before or since. Plangent, plaintive, wistful, wild. Part, it seemed, of an infinite melody, and the man and his tin whistle simply opened the window to it for a while and it entered from the universe into that dismal tunnel on that dank day.

For us. Specifically for us. He played for us.

How long did we stand there? It might have been five minutes or several hours.

A roaring behind us caused me to turn as a boy on a skateboard tore past and crashed into the underpass. As my eyes followed him, I saw that there was no figure sitting under the lamp any more, no whistler. Only the hooded boy careering down and deafening us. And then he left the far end, and there again was the drip drip from the stalactites.

And we went back home for tea.

The Cares of the World

Cleo walked through the Old Castle Arcade as she had many times, but today, because of all that had happened, she was watching people, not looking at the shops. Today she observed how they walked, what made one person's gait distinctive. Sometimes she tried to mimic a person for a few steps, but felt she might be caught out and thought to be mocking them.

Then she noticed a pair of green trousers that were utterly still in the midst of the flow of people. Her eyes travelled upwards. A young bespectacled man in a green fleece was standing staring into a window, motionless. She followed his gaze. It was a shop of antiques or repro furniture and objects. On a slender, octagonal, occasional table stood a small bronze figure. A girl, head thrown back, hair streaming, arms flung out. A transport of abandoned happiness. Cleo was captivated. The figure seemed to radiate and expand and subsume her. Then she became aware of silence. Tearing her eyes away, she looked around. The Arcade was deserted. No young, green-clad man, no shoppers. No-one.

As unease started to permeate, she felt impelled to look back at the figure. That figure of joy. What did she care?

Like one in a trance, in a state of suspended time, Cleo drifted through the door of the shop and found herself picking up the figurine. £27.68 said the label underneath. What a curious sum! She had at least thirty pounds in her purse. Then a crash out in the Arcade attracted her attention, and she moved out to see what it was. As she did, a voice behind her in the depths of the shop, arresting yet ancient, cried out 'That is stealing. Be warned, the police are summoned.'

She turned to protest, but another voice from the Arcade said 'Put it down.' And that voice carried such authority that she immediately obeyed. The speaker was a police officer with penetrating eyes. They transfixed her, so that she did not move as he took her left hand with his right and placed his left on her right shoulder. The next minute they were dancing, first sedately, formally, then with increasing wildness. His eyes never left her. They bumped into sofas, collided with chairs, smashed into cabinets. Ornaments went flying.

As suddenly as he had begun, the policeman stopped. Breathless, she was directly in front of the shop owner, elderly and properly suited, who was crying with laughter, his eyes wrinkled up and dripping, his cheeks puce, his fists dug into his stomach.

Her breathing gradually slowed. The old man's laughter subsided. The policeman had vanished. Cleo found herself proffering three ten-pound notes. The old man said, wiping his eyes, 'Take her. She's yours.'

Cleo picked up the figure, and as she went, left the £30 on the little table.

Out in the Arcade, everyone seemed to be doing comical walks, and she chuckled to herself all the way to the Cadena Café, where she bought a cappuccino and a slice of cherry cake. The little statue of Thalia, muse of comedy, stood on the table in front of her, arms flung out throwing off the cares of the world while Cleo devoured them with the utmost delight.

Mustard

Oliphant walked into the Police Station, feeling guilty and puzzled. The guilt was ridiculous. He ignored it. The puzzlement was understandable. When they rang him and said a box had been found and handed in which had his name on it, he could think of nothing he'd lost that fitted the description. But here he was, passport and utility bill in hand to prove he was who he said he was and lived where he did.

The box was about two foot long and a foot square in the other dimensions. He'd never seen it in his life before. It was wooden. It had his name engraved on the top. There weren't many Oliphant Goss-Custards in the town. He was unique, of that he was sure. So he took the box. It was heavy. He managed to carry it to the car, heaved it into the boot and looked at it. Good craftsmanship. A keyhole with a polished brass surround. How was he to open it? It would be a terrible shame to damage the box by forcing it.

So he half-heartedly simply tried lifting the lid. It swung open easily. Inside there was a small creature waving what looked like a sandwich at him.

'I need some mustard,' it said.

'Mustard?' Oliphant repeated stupidly.

'You have a shop. It's a General Stores. You must sell mustard. I only need a little bit.' The creature looked like what Oliphant imagined a goblin would look like. He gawped.

'Stop gawping,' said the creature. 'Just because you've never seen a live goblin before. I'll have you know we're pretty similar to you, except that most goblins, I have to assume, prefer ham sandwiches without mustard, which is why they gave me this.' He waved the sandwich disdainfully. 'I can't eat it. I must have mustard. I'll sit inside.' And the goblin leaped out of the box and sprang over the back seat in one fluent movement.

Oliphant had little choice but to drive to his shop, where his apprentice, John Smith, was holding the fort. As he got out of the car, the goblin jumped onto his shoulder and kicked him hard. 'Get a move on, can't you?' he said in his ear.

Oliphant told the astonished John Smith to fetch mustard, which he did. The goblin opened it, stuck a bony finger in, and smeared it all over his ham sandwich. He ate it in silence.

'Ah!' he said, when he had finished. 'That's more like it. Here you are then, Mr Goss-Custard. Be seeing you!' With which he leaped from his shoulder and vanished out of the door.

Oliphant looked at the scrap of paper the goblin had given him. It read, in a spidery hand, "16, 18, 26, 38, 44, lucky stars 8, 10. EuroMillions today. Treasure guaranteed." Well, actually it said "Teaser granted," but goblins aren't known for their spelling ability.

'Stop gawping, boy!' he said to John Smith. 'I'm popping round to the newsagents. See that this floor is swept by the time I come back.'

And off he went to put the numbers into the lottery.

So, did he win, you ask? Not exactly. But the paramedic did, who first arrived on the scene after Oliphant, dreaming of becoming rich beyond his wildest dreams, was hit by an articulated lorry he failed to notice when crossing the road.

How to Write a Poem

There is a ladder leaning up against a house. The top is resting on a first floor window sill. The window is open.

Joe walks past, not underneath the ladder, around it, his head screwing round as he passes to look up at the window. He continues on to the little park just up the road, where he sits himself on a bench in the sun. Try as he might to compose a poem in his mind, which was his intention, the memory of the ladder won't leave him alone. Anyone could climb it, climb through the window, into somebody's secret world.

What does he know of the house, he asks himself? He passes it most days. It is Number 37, proclaimed by the tarnished brass numerals screwed to the door, a door once white, but now peeling in parts and splashed with grime from passing traffic. The ground floor windows have net curtains, he recalls.

Once when he passed, he saw a rolled-up newspaper partly sticking out of the letter-box. In the park that day, he determined to remove the paper if he could on his way back, but when he got there, it had vanished. He was relieved, for he didn't really understand why he wanted the newspaper. Unwittingly, the inhabitant of the house had spared himself the inconvenience of losing the paper, but also rescued him, Joe, from committing a flagrant act of theft. But now, today, there is this ladder...

What if he climbs the ladder, enters the open window? He would not be exactly breaking and entering, since the window is open, but it's not the behaviour one would expect of a decent honest citizen. And what if he encountered the house's owner inside? He might take outrage at the liberty. Probably would.

But then, what if he finds the owner lying on the floor, felled by a heart attack, or having tripped and banged his head? Won't Joe then be a hero, calling the emergency services, saving his life? Looked at like that, it seems entirely proper that he should at least climb and look through the window to see if indeed someone is lying unconscious on the floor. A responsible act.

But what if when he looks there is nobody there on the floor? What should he do then? He ponders on this a while, while the wind wafts leaves about in the sun's beams and a blackbird sings.

After some minutes, having accepted that he is not going to dream up a poem this morning. Joe resolves that on his way back, he will climb the ladder and peep inside. Then, at that time, depending on what he sees, only then will he decide what to do next. Yes. That is a good and responsible plan.

He leaves the park and walks back down the road to Number 37. The ladder is still there, still leaning. But there is nothing for it lean against. No window sill. No window. No house. The ladder leans against nothing beside a deserted plot on which scrubby weeds are growing.

Unable to take this in, Joe climbs the ladder anyway. It feels perfectly steady and stable. As his head reaches the top, it passes through something, and he finds himself in another place.

He looks down and can't see his body and legs. He takes another step upwards. Some of his torso and arms appear. He steps up once again, sits on the edge and swings his legs up from wherever else they were. From here, now, there is no sign of the ladder or where it has been.

Joe looks around. He seems to be in another park. Trees, shrubs, flowers, all look different somehow. Joe thinks he would like a cup of tea and a custard cream. Over there is a bench and a picnic table. He sits on the bench. In front of him there is indeed a steaming cup and a biscuit. So he drinks and nibbles.

As he does, he is aware of the sounds around – a blackbird singing, a distant dog barking, rustling leaves.

No, it's not rustling, it's a hissing. White sound, growing louder, coming closer. He turns.

The jaws part, the fangs drip, the snake eyes pierce through him as he is dragged into the mouth, the lower jaw dislocating to take his bulk. He begins a terrible slide, indescribable.

Indescribable it may be, but brief. In a moment he is out, out in the sunshine. Number 37 stands before him, there is no ladder. Above, the snake's tail whips away up into the sky and out of sight.

And there, he realises with a start, there in his mind, is a poem, ready formed. A haiku. He recites it to a passing cat, who looks the other way.

> *Oh, what is life but*
> *A game of snakes and ladders*
> *And a blackbird's song?*

Sausages

One afternoon in October, his mum's freshly-made mustard on the noontide boiled beef and carrots catapulted the normally comatose Flann into action. He went for a walk around the town. And so he passed the Gate. There sat Osmund, the Gatekeeper in his little shelter, warming his toes by a glowing brazier on which he was cooking some sausages.

To his surprise, Flann caught a thought as he passed, a thought that could only come from the Gatekeeper himself. *Of course!* the thought went. *He would do. Too dumb to question, too lazy to complain.* Flann was in no doubt the Gatekeeper's thought applied to him.

Maybe that's so, thought Flann in his turn, though he had no idea what Osmund, the Gatekeeper, thought him suitable for. What he did know was that, lunch notwithstanding, the sausages smelled splendid, and he tried sending a thought back to the Gatekeeper.

'Oi!' called out Osmund, 'you want a sausage, boy?'

It had worked! The sausage was hot. Flann juggled it from hand to hand and blew on it.

'You ever thought of settling down, boy?' said Osmund.

Flann looked about for something to settle down on, but there was only the one chair in the Gatekeeper's shelter, currently occupied by a lot of Gatekeeper.

'You should take a job,' said Osmund. 'Lad like you needs a career. Bit of stability in your life. And as it happens, I'm due for retirement. Fancy a life of Gatekeeping, eh? Good, steady work, pay's not bad, free sausages...'

He talked on and on until he convinced himself it was probably the most fulfilling and desirable job in the world. Remarkable feat for a man with almost no imagination.

As you probably know, the post of Gatekeeper is traditionally passed down in the family, father to son. Lack of imagination is a necessary prerequisite, an inherited gene in the right family. Osmund, not through want of trying, had seven daughters, and his wife had called time.

As it happened, Flann needed no more inducement than free sausages, and so, in due course, he was officially appointed Gatekeeper in a small ceremony involving the Mayor, Osmund, Osmund's seven daughters, in the vain hope that Flann might take a shine to one of them, and Flann's mum.

The rules and responsibilities of the Gatekeeper were few:

1. The Gate shall remain locked at all times.

2. Nobody shall be allowed through without a pass signed by the Town Clerk or a Justice of the Peace.

For the first two weeks, no-one went through the Gate. Following complaints, Osmund was dug out of retirement to explain to Flann that rule 1 meant, yes, the Gate was always to be locked, except when someone with a valid pass wanted to go through.

Thereafter there was a steady trickle of perhaps one or two a day through the Gate. Meanwhile, Flann ate sausages and grew plumper.

After a couple of months, it dawned on him that all those who went through the Gate went in the same direction – from the Town to the Outside World. He pondered this for a few weeks more, and then decided to examine the Gate.

It was wooden, very solid, some eight foot high. You could squint through the keyhole, but it didn't tell you much.

Flann went back to his sausages. Being his birthday, his mother had brought him a present of her frisky little mustard, and his life gained a new dimension. Perhaps the events weren't connected, but for the first time in his life, Flann's natural curiosity, normally barely perceptible, began to peek its little head above the parapet.

A flamboyant gentleman wearing an immaculate purple velvet suit with an orange chrysanthemum in his button-hole, waved a document in front of Flann. 'My pass,' he declared. Flann might have thought it looked very like his mum's bus pass, but he was consumed by the spark of curiosity wondering if the chrysanthemum was real or artificial, and so he unlocked the Gate for the gentleman without a murmur.

And then that cheeky imp of curiosity suddenly made him decide to look out of the Gate to see where the gent went and what the World Outside actually looked like. Just a quick peek. Why not?

What he saw was a small encampment of colourful tents, and a circle of folk sitting on logs around a cheerful camp-fire, over which a stew pot was bubbling.

The man in the velvet suit, meanwhile, walked straight past them, along a path and over a nearby hill out of sight and out of the story.

Flann was transfixed. He sneaked through the gate and sidled over to the stew pot. The people sat motionless, watching him. He leant over to smell the aromas, deep, savoury, enticing, drawing in great breaths of contentment and anticipation. Were he to ask nicely, he thought, maybe they would let him try a taste.

He withdrew his head and turned around. The circle was empty. Not a soul – except he could just see the last one disappearing through the Gate. As he hastened towards it, he heard the familiar squeak as the key turned in the lock and bolts slid into place.

Back in the town, Osmund, the ex-Gatekeeper, was finding life at home unbearable, what with his seven squabbling daughters, and was only too glad to come out of retirement and resume his post.

And legend has it that Flann's mum never had the heart to make mustard again.

Tall tales from the pub

Duck's Dream

The lunchtime trade was over. Under the sleepy sun outside the Danbury Arms, beside the minuscule village green and pint-sized pond, nothing stirred but the pages of a forgotten newspaper, dancing to an idle breeze, and the village duck. He stomped about poking through the grass in case there was a dropped chip or lettuce leaf. When he reached the newspaper, he stopped. What caught his eye was a terrible tale of abuse of expenses, of an MP claiming for a duck house in the middle of his pond. A castle of a duck house, a palace, a five-star Astoria of a duck house. Danbury Duck was transfixed. It was for this he had been hatched. No more squatting in the long grass, rain or shine. A roof over his head and who knows what luxury inside.

All afternoon he swam in small circles round his little puddle, and thought and thought. By the time the first evening drinkers arrived, he knew what the secret was. Money. He needed money. A lot of it.

Two young men in suits, reps unwinding after a day's selling, sat themselves at the table by the pond with beer and crisps.

'I'm chucking it in,' said one. 'Getting a job in London. That's where the money is.'

'Come on Dunc,' said the other. 'Think of the commuting.'

'Sod that,' said Dunc, 'It'll be peanuts to what I do now.'

It was all he needed to hear. Danbury Duck knew he too must head for London. It was where the money was. The money for his duck heaven.

And so, next morning, Danbury tied a crust of bread and a chunk of cheese into a spotted handkerchief, and set off on his waddle to the great city.

Before long, he heard a voice say 'Excuse me!' and turned to see a fox, who promptly took him in his jaws.

'Oi!' cried Danbury. 'That's not fair. You didn't give me a chance.'

The fox put him down. 'Look,' he said, 'this isn't a game. There aren't rules. I mean, if I gave you a chance, you would simply fly out of reach.'

'That's a good idea,' said Danbury. 'I didn't think of that.' And he flew into a tree.

The fox prowled round, reproaching himself for not listening to his mother, who had constantly exhorted him not to be so polite. Eventually he tired, and went off to look for easier pickings.

Danbury flew down and resumed his trek. After a few hours, he stopped and ate his bread and cheese. A lorry drew up alongside him and the driver leaned out. ''Ere mate,' he said, 'Want a lift?'

'London?' asked Danbury.

'Sure thing, ducky,' said the driver. 'Hop in.'

So Danbury climbed into the cab while the driver embarked on a lengthy saga detailing his marital troubles. After his meal, Danbury found drowsiness overtaking him. He drifted off, dreaming of money and his destined designer duck house.

When he awoke, something was different. The driver was still droning on. It wasn't that. It was the road. Whereas they had been on a main highway, as befits a road to London, now the lorry was bouncing along a country lane.

'Excuse me,' Danbury was about to say, when he caught sight of a pile of leaflets on the seat beside him.

"Burke's Ducks" they said. "Quality suppliers to the nation's finest gastronomic emporia. Only state-of-the-art hygienic intensive rearing."

A shiver ran down Danbury's spine. He was heading for some duck concentration camp, not London at all, at least not alive. What was he to do? Then he remembered the lesson the fox had taught him: ducks can fly. So he flew. Given the confines of the cab, it was more frantic flapping than flight, and it terrified the driver, who tried simultaneously to catch Danbury, avoid his wings, and keep the lorry on the road. To this, he added winding his window down in the hope that the duck would fly out.

It was the driving that suffered. The lorry veered gracefully off the road, down a bank and tumbled into a lake they were passing. Danbury escaped through the window. He landed some distance away, and watched the lorry sink rapidly below the surface. He watched bubbles break on the surface. He watched them stop.

'What was all that about?' Danbury turned to see who was speaking. A duck was swimming towards him. A brown duck. An irresistibly plain and drab duck. A female duck. Danbury waggled his tail.

'Race you to the island,' she said, and they were off, kicking up spray, half flying, half paddling. And as his feet flapped and his wings beat, he knew for certain he had found his riches, his dream, and money didn't come into it at all. Who needs a duck house when you've got an island in a lake, and a drab companion?

St John and the Maiden

'Did I tell you about St John Ferret, the most evil boy in my school?' Piers adjusted his fundament on the barstool and swigged his pint of Spotted Hen, confident he had our attention. Which indeed he did. Including a stranger seated on the stool beside me, a depressed-looking interloper. But we are an inclusive bunch in the Green Man.

'School bully,' Piers went on. 'Made Flashman seem a cissy. If you had buckteeth, or a lisp, or red hair, or your balls were a bit late dropping, St John would be merciless. He would make you feel smaller than a worm in seconds. At least, so I observed. Of course, he didn't bother me. I was, after all, Piers.

'Teachers weren't exempt either. I remember old Dykes, our English teacher. Started banging on about Wordsworth or some such fellow. St John took exception. Fixed him with his eyes, a special look that said, "I am but a poor innocent simply trying to make sense of the world," but also said, "I can see into your soul. Be very scared."

'"Please... *sir*," St John said, with an unnatural pause before the "sir." "Please... *sir*, what is Poetry *for*?"

'Old Dykes started to pontificate in fine form, quoting this, citing that. St John simply sat stock still, silent, and looked at him with that look. Dykes began to stumble a little. Still St John looked, looked and watched him as he began to fluster and flounder and blanch and colour.

'And then St John spoke. "Ha ha," he said, completely cold and flat. "Ha ha," like that. Old Dykes stopped, his posture a picture of pathos. And the other boys started giggling. They couldn't help it. Not me, of course. I looked on in moral outrage as Old Dykes' face crumpled and tears began to creep down his cheeks.

'It was clinical on St John's part. He was honing his edge, I realise. Old Dykes resigned the next day, and spent his remaining years in a monastery, I believe.

'Understand me, chaps, St John never did anything brutal. Not personally. His methods were psychological, and, as I said, clinical. And very effective. If he happened to encounter a particularly obtuse victim who remained immune to his rapiers, he had a number of henchboys, roughly cylindrical in shape, with fists like ham hocks and brains like peas, who were only too happy to put the occasional boot in, and who administered any subsequent punishment that might be deemed apt. Not St John himself. He, like Macavity, would have been somewhere else at the time.

'So, my jolly drinking companions, you can understand my total astonishment when, yesterday, I was passing through a desolate building site the other side of town, and there I saw him, at the wheel of a bulldozer. And in front of the bulldozer was a comely young maiden securely tied to stakes driven into the ground. St John was driving the bulldozer straight at her, his face completely expressionless. He who never sullied his hands with violence. I recognised him straight away, all these years later.

'"Hey, St John!" I yelled.

'He turned those eyes upon me. I expected that look, the one that reduced old Dykes to a blubbering heap, but no. There was a blank stare, as though he couldn't even see me, as if I wasn't there. I waved a hand. "It's Piers," I said, in case he couldn't remember me.

'Gradually I saw his eyes begin to focus. They looked puzzled. "Hey, St John," I said, "you're about to run a fair maiden over. Not a good idea, old chap."

'He cast his gaze about and saw her in her tethered state before the bulldozer. "Do you know her?" I asked, but at that moment, the maiden stopped screaming. Did I mention that she was screaming the whole time? Up to then, that is? Very ear-splittingly.

'"St John, you bastard," she spat at him, "stop being a prize idiot. It was only a sonnet."

'Well, it took me a while, but the Piers charm managed to calm them down. I took them off to a local hostelry and plied them with restorative draughts. Meanwhile I weaselled the story out of them.

'The maiden in question was apparently somewhat entranced by our St John and his evil aura, and had written him a poem. A sonnet. Fourteen lines of immortal verse. St John, as we have heard, does not care for poetry. Hence the stakes and bulldozer. Natural reaction, when you think about it.'

I saw Piers was looking at the stranger seated on the bar stool beside me. There seemed to be compassion in his eyes. Not like Piers at all.

'Your round, I think,' he said to the chap, then turned to the rest of us. 'May I introduce St John Ferret, my dears? He is going to buy us all a drink. Aren't you, St John.'

And the stranger did exactly that, after which he slunk out of the door. Oh, Piers was in fine fettle that evening.

Fish and Chips

We were discussing the merits of the chippies in town. General consensus was that Poisson n' Frites was best. I disagreed. The Jolly Friar had the edge, I averred, and was where I would drop in on my way home.

'Ah,' cried Piers from his favourite bar-stool, 'that reminds me of seeing Pasolini's *Canterbury Tales* back in the 70s at the Odeon.'

'What's that got to do with the price of mushy peas?' the rest of us chorused. Piers can be elliptical.

He was undaunted. 'I realised there was something odd,' he went on, 'when what was on the screen was being reflected in what appeared to be a circular mirror in the row in front of me.

'It was only when the usherette appeared post-Pearl and Dean and he got up to buy an ice-cream, that I realised what it was: a tonsure, doubtless newly shaven and polished.'

He paused for dramatic effect, but met only with puzzlement from us regulars. Until light struck me. You have to think cryptic clues with Piers. 'It was my mention of the Jolly Friar!' I cried. 'Friars, monks, shaved heads, tonsures!'

Piers smiled patronisingly. 'Just so,' he said. 'A monk. A Grey Friar, to be precise, as evinced by the colour of his habit. Not what you expect in a provincial flea-pit. Perhaps he was there attracted by the Friar's Tale in the Canterbury Tales, to see if it was realistic.'

'That film was a bit rude, wasn't it?' sniggered Algy.

Piers silenced him with a withering wave of his glass. 'My dear Algy,' he said. 'it is an art film. But that is not relevant. What is deeply significant is a monk buying and eating an ice-cream – a raspberry ripple, by the way.

'For, in the midst of the Miller's Tale – you know, the bit about the miller's daughter and a window and a red hot poker – at that exact moment, there was an extraordinary sound from the seat in front of me, a cross between a gully-emptier and a cat throwing up a fur ball, and the tonsure slid out of my sight. None of my business, I thought at the time. The film played on to its end, the credits rolled and the lights came up.

'It was then the poor chap was noticed. Face purple. Dead as a dodo. The cinema people shooed everyone home quick-smart, trying to downplay the incident, but I insisted on sticking around. Being directly behind the deceased, I argued, I might be able to give useful information to the medics and possibly police when they arrived.

'And arrive they did! It was quickly clear to the doctor who pronounced Father Whatsit lifeless, that he had been poisoned.'

Again Piers paused for effect. Algy muttered, 'Gosh!' and I think he spoke for us all. After a moment's quiet contemplation on the transitory nature of existence, another beam of light smote my brain. 'Poison in the raspberry ripple!' I cried, feeling like Sherlock Holmes and Miss Marple rolled into one.

'Exactly so,' said Piers. 'The next thing I knew,' he continued, 'I was being bundled into a police car and ended up in an interview room. Chilling, I can tell you.

'Why had I sat directly behind Father Doodah, they asked me? Because the usherette showed me to that row, I told them.

'Had I looked at the usherette? Would I recognise her again? Sure, I said, I particularly noticed that she had very big feet, clad in flat, leather sandals, and that there was stubble on her chin.

'Was she the same usherette who sold the ice-creams? Yes, I was sure she was.

'Did she pick the raspberry ripple and give it to Father Thing, or did he choose which one to take? Haven't a clue, I told them.

'And then they started on more obscure questions. Had I ever been to Peru? Did I know anyone who had? What did I know of the Order of Hermit Friars Sinister, sometimes called the Fish Friars?

'Well, these were easy enough to answer. No, no and nothing. But what were they after? I was deeply puzzled, I must say.

'Then they asked me where I'd been to school, and after that their tone changed considerably. Suddenly I clearly became beyond suspicion. They even started being chatty. The poison, they told me, was an alkaloid derived from an exceedingly rare fern only found in the high Andes. It was tasteless and had no effect for an hour or so after ingestion, after which decline and death were sudden and inevitable. They suspected, as indeed did you,' – he pointed his beer glass at me – 'that it was contained in the raspberry ripple, though they had thought for a moment that I might have administered it through an hypodermic syringe from my seat directly behind Father Whatsit – until they learned where I'd been educated, of course.'

Algy, who considers himself a prosecuting council manqué, piped up. 'How,' he demanded, 'could they possibly have identified such an obscure poison so quickly?'

Piers waved his empty glass dismissively. 'The Police work in mysterious ways,' he said, and tapped the side of his nose with a forefinger. 'But they did tell me a few tantalising things about the Fish Friars. A fanatical order, they said, solitary, sworn to annihilation of what they considered phony Friars, top of which list were the Franciscans, of whom Father Tiddley-Pom was one.

'Yes,' he repeated, 'mysterious are the ways of our boys in blue. But they are fair. Why, they even sent out for some fish and chips during our interview. Very civilised. From the Codfather, of course. Best I ever tasted.'

Algy had not given up his cross examination. 'Piers...' he began.

Piers pressed his glass into Algy's hand. 'A pint of Shaggy Dog, thank you, Algy,' he said.

Algy blustered. 'No, no.... Oh, all right then. No, Piers, I wanted to ask you, where did you go to school?'

'Why, Greyfriars,' said Piers.

There was a pause. Then a third ray of light struck me. 'Piers,' I said, 'Greyfriars is where Billy Bunter went to school, isn't it?'

'Is it?' he said.

'Piers,' I went on, 'is there a single grain of truth in your tale?'

Piers took the pint that Algy passed him and drank deep. Wiping his upper lip, he said, 'Why, of course there is. I did get thrown out of the Odeon during The

Canterbury Tales, and it did involve a Raspberry Ripple and an usherette, but, I swear, it was my chum Reginald Fox-Silver who did it, not me. I've never spoken to him since. And I did have the best ever fish and chips from the Codfather, so there.' He supped on, silent at last.

The Milkmaid

I was having a quiet pint in the Three Geese when Tristram came over, looking shady.

'Guy,' he said, flicking his eyes round to see if he could be overheard, 'just between you and me, tonight's the night.'

'For what?'

'He's planning to do the deed.' Tristram tapped the side of his nose.

'What are you on about,' I said. 'Who? What deed?'

'My friend Norman,' he said. And the penny dropped. He's been going on about Norman for weeks. Tristram goes up to London a lot – don't ask why. When he's there he stays with this Norman, who's a bit of an odd-ball, if you ask me. Rather obsessional and reclusive.

'Norman's got it bad,' Tristram told me some time back. 'He's fallen in love with this milkmaid in the V&A.'

'Don't talk cobblers, Tristram,' I said. 'The V&A's a museum, not a farm.'

Tristram explained.

'Norman,' he said, 'is a bit of an art freak. The old stuff. Rembrandt and that. Well, as it happens, there's a big exhibition of Dutch masters at the V&A. They've brought in stuff from all over, and Norman is pretty much a fixture there. He takes a camping stool in so he can be comfy.

'He's particularly smitten by Vermeer's painting *The Milkmaid*. There's a bit of the Mona Lisa about her, he says. Inscrutable. Reckons he can read her, though. He reckons – and this is the weird bit – he reckons she talks to him. Not out loud. But he says she moves her lips, and he can tell what she's saying. She says she's trapped there, that she longs to be released, and – get this – that she loves him. I tell him he's delusional and spends too much time on his own. But he is adamant. He knows. And when Norman knows something, he knows it.

'Anyway, I went to have a look at the floozie. Fine painting. Good beefy rustic lass. Not the sort I would think Norman would go for. I'll tell you Guy – and don't breathe a word of this – he says he's going to nick her. It's absurd. He's constitutionally incapable, if you ask me. But he's dead set.'

And now, in the Three Geese, Tristram was telling me Norman was going to steal Vermeer's *Milkmaid* tonight.

'How?' I said.

'Search me,' said Tristram. 'However, there's no way he'll manage it. These places are bristling with security. It'll end in tears, believe me.'

Next day it was all over the news. The milkmaid was gone. Not, as you might imagine, the painting, but the figure from the painting. The room was still there, the jug suspended in mid-air with milk still pouring from it – but no milkmaid. They wheeled out the pundits to pronounce upon it, even an ex-art thief, but none of them had a clue.

The day after that, they were further dumbfounded. In the adjoining gallery, in Rembrandt's *Night Watch*, the night watch went missing. All of them. As though they had never been in the painting. The talk was of nothing else, particularly in the Three Geese. Tristram announced he was going up to London. Urgent business, he said, but I knew he was going to see Norman.

The following day, the mystery deepened even further. The Milkmaid reappeared in her painting. So too did the Night Watch in theirs. It was as though nothing had happened, though some alleged the milkmaid's expression was more sullen than before. The media rapidly lost interest.

A few days after that, I was in the Three Geese when Tristram came over, back from his "business" in London.

'He's gone,' he said. 'Norman's vanished. Disparu.'

'Holiday?' I suggested.

'Norman doesn't do holidays,' said Tristram. 'No. He's gone. I'll tell you what I've been doing. Spending a lot of time in the V&A. I thought, the answer must lie there. I've been studying the catalogue and the pictures, and I think I've found what happened to him. Do you know Hieronymus Bosch?'

'No,' I said.

'Do you know his Last Judgement?'

'No.'

Tristram looked crestfallen. 'It's very famous,' he said. 'Anyway, I compared the picture with the photo in the catalogue. It's a triptych, you know. The right-hand panel shows wicked souls being punished in hell. And I reckon there's another figure in that panel now, one that isn't in the photo. And I reckon it looks like…'

He stopped. I was looking at him pityingly. 'Dear, oh dear, Tristram,' I said. 'You're talking cobblers, you know that? Let me buy you a pint.'

'But…' he started. 'Oh, never mind. Make it a whisky, Guy. A double.'

Revised Version

'Where are you from?' I asked.

'Just the other side of that door,' he said, pointing to the entrance to the pub. I laughed.

'Ha ha,' I said. 'And before that?'

'There was no before.' He looked serious. Again I had the odd feeling I knew him from somewhere.

It had seemed that way when he first came over a few minutes earlier. The bar was quiet. I'd popped in for a pint before lunch and a glance at the paper. I didn't really notice him come in and order a drink, only when he was standing by the table.

'May I join you?' he had said.

'Sure,' I replied. 'Be my guest. Ah, you're on the Bosun's Revenge too, I see. Fine pint. Distinctive colour.'

'Of course,' he said.

And now here he was claiming there was no "before". Curious.

'You mean you popped into existence just outside the pub a few minutes back?' I asked. 'Sort of fully formed?'

'More or less,' he said.

'But you have memories, right? You must have done something for the past thirty odd years?'

'Thirty-two,' he said. Same age as me.

'There you are,' I said. 'Thirty-two years of past.'

'Well, no,' he said. 'Not exactly. More like ten minutes.'

I took a good swig of Bosun's Revenge. He didn't look like a nutter. Regular features, bit leaner and fitter than me, no bags under the eyes. He seemed perfectly and healthily normal.

'Right,' I pondered. 'You're thirty-two years old and you have no memory of it. Pretty serious amnesia, if you don't mind me saying.'

'Oh, naturally I have memories,' he said. 'Only they aren't mine.'

'Sure, sure,' I said. 'So whose are they?'

'Yours,' he said. That floored me.

'Mine?' I tried.

'Yours,' he repeated. This was getting nowhere.

'Look,' I said, 'are you trying to be funny or something? I mean, I just came in here for a quiet pint and a look at the paper, and you...'

'Surely you were expecting me?' he interrupted. He looked at his watch. 'This is the right time and place. And the right day, I'm sure.'

'For what?' I cried. 'I don't know you!'

'Not specifically, you don't, of course,' he said. 'But this is the planned time for your update.'

'What?'

'And you must realise that a firmware upgrade wouldn't be enough this time. You've let your body, your hardware, go to pot, technology's advanced since your last upgrade, and so, according to the terms of the contract, you're eligible for a replacement model. That's me.'

'Hang on, hang on,' I said. 'Let me see if I understand you. you're saying you're going to replace me? You're the new Simon Barker. Well, what about me? I take exception to all this. I'm not ready to pop my clogs yet. I've got things to do...' I tailed off. He was shaking his head.

'It's OK, I'll do all those things. You've nothing to worry about; you're simply decommissioned. If you're lucky, you'll be refurbished for a lower category region. Recycling's high on priorities these days.'

'No,' I said. 'No, no no. Go away. Leave me alone. Enough!'

'I can't do that. It's all part of a rolling programme to replace everyone by new and improved models.'

'Models! I'm not a model,' I blazed. 'I'm a person. With rights!'

'I know, I know you think that,' he said. 'It's a delusion. That's one of the design bugs that are addressed in us new models. Current versions are undelusional, seventy percent healthier, much improved will-power, lower aggression. You've seen the advertisements.'

'No, I haven't. What advertisements?'

'Yes, you have,' he said. 'For the FRC. It's in your memories. I should know.' He tapped his head.

'What's the FRC?' I said.

He fell silent and looked long and hard at me. 'You really don't know, do you?' he said eventually. 'The *Freebody Robotics Corporation*. This is odd.'

'You're telling me,' I said, but he put up a hand to stop me.

'Just hang on a minute,' he said. 'I'm accessing the Troubleshooting Guide.'

What do you say when something like this happens? I mean, it doesn't happen, not in my world. What do you do? How do you make sense of it? My head was aching.

'I think I've got it,' he said. 'Buried away in the FAQ. *Frequently Asked Questions*,' he explained, obviously doubting my ability to understand any acronyms. 'In rare circumstances, it appears, a human is fabricated but the original life-form fails to be removed. You *are* actually human, is that right?'

I nodded, bereft of speech.

'That means... Hey!' he cried, holding his hand up again. 'Is there another bar here?'

I pointed mutely.

'Ah,' he said. 'I wonder...' He walked over and flung open the door to the Snug.

'So there you are!' I heard a voice from within the Snug exclaim. 'I was wondering where you'd got to.'

The voice sounded terribly like mine.

The Museum of Monstrosities

Do you remember Charles Flood? I expect you do, that bucolic, bon viveur and bibliomaniac who bought up an old pumping station near Skegness and turned it into the Museum of Monstrosities back in the nineties. You must remember that. The outrage, the righteous indignation that made the headlines for weeks. Eminent historians, archaeologists and heaven knows who all crying out to preserve a decaying building "as it was" as though it were an Etruscan temple or a Stone Age hill fort. I suspect most of them had no idea what a pumping station pumped or why, and had never seen one.

Well, whether you remember him or not, I ran into Charles last week, and he, after I reminded him who *I* was, suggested we had a drink together at the Bosom of Abraham and caught up. By which he meant he'd talk and I'd buy. I asked him about the Museum.

'My boy,' he snorted, in that way of his, 'they paid me to blow it up.'

I had visited the Museum of Monstrosities shortly after it opened, and only a few exhibits stick in my mind. I wish they didn't. There was a mummified monkey with two heads, I remember, a strange beast that seemed to be part bird, part fish and part dog, which I suspect was a taxidermist's joke, a bottle of formaldehyde containing a tapeworm quarter of a mile long that had been extracted from the gut of some poor unfortunate, that sort of thing. It made me feel sick, and I remember coming away with the feeling that I'd be happy never to visit it again. I suggested to Charles Flood that surely such repulsive gruesomeness would make the Museum a magnet for tourists and a great success.

'You'd think so, my boy,' he bellowed, 'and for a while it was. But there was Agamemnon and Tinkerbell, and then the flood. Could have been publicity, but what eye-catching headlines did it get in the press?'

'"Flood at Flood's"?' I proposed.

He snorted again. 'Too subtle by miles for the local press,' he said. 'More like "Monstrosities Threaten Skegness – will this kill tourism?" We fought, we argued, we got the best lawyers, but in the end we lost and bang! The Museum blown to smithereens.'

I said I failed to see why such an extreme measure was called for, and he shook his head at my dimwittedness.

'Agamemnon and Tinkerbell, my boy, as I just said if you bothered to listen. That'll cost you another double scotch.'

After I'd placed it in front of him, he carried on. 'Aggers and Tinkers and their benighted offspring started menacing bathers.'

I said I might be an imbecile, but it still didn't make sense.

Sighing, he spoke to me as to a retarded five-year-old.

'Pumping station,' he said. 'Pumps water from River Thingy up to reservoir at Whatsit. Or it used to until the 1960s when they found a cheaper way to do it. Then, when the Museum is only a year or so old, for some reason unexplained, the old pumps suddenly leap into action again. Pipes up to reservoir long ago disconnected, so the River Thingy gets pumped into my Museum of Marvellous Monstrosities. I suspect it was sabotage. I suspect that poncy, pince-nez-wearing architectural historian chappie, you know the one I mean?'

'And?' I interrupted.

'And what?' he said.

'What happened as a result of the flood?'

'I told you,' he barked. 'Agamemnon and Tinkerbell escaped.'

'Charles,' I screamed, 'for the love of Mike who or what are Agamemnon and Tinkerbell?'

'Were,' corrected Charles. 'They've certainly rotted away by now. They were the stars, my favourite exhibit. Not monstrous, I admit, but very clever for the time. This was the 90s remember. Invented by the inventor chappie, you know, the bonkers one you see on the box. Electronic goldfish. Never need feeding. Brilliant. But come the flood, they escaped. Made their way to the sea. Salt water triggered something, and next thing you know they're reproducing, spawning all over the place, and they seem to have taken against mankind and started chomping swimmers' toes and fingers. Panic widespread. Anger. Tourists keep away in droves. Bad news.'

'But why did you have to blow up the Museum?' I asked.

'Oh, that was nothing to do with the goldfish. The water got to the mummified monkey with two heads, and the cacodemons, and goblins and sooterkins and so on. Moment they became rehydrated, they came back to life in a manner of speaking and started haunting the place. You ventured in after the flood had subsided, you came out gibbering and frothing at the mouth, totally mad. Nasty bit of work. Drain on the health services. Paid me to go in with the gelignite and blow the place sky high.' He held his empty glass out for a refill.

'Gosh,' I said. 'And what did you do after that?'

'I got a franchise selling candyfloss on the sea-front if you must know. Got to do my bit to bring tourists back. Very dull in the winter months. Retired now.'

'Well I never,' I said. 'My life since we last met has been very different, but equally exciting, I would say...'

He rose to his feet, drained his Scotch, and extended a hand.

'Got to go, my boy. Another time maybe.'

And off he strode, the bar door swinging behind him.

Emmenthal Crackers

'I am your Cheese Fairy,' she said. 'Is it cool if I sit down?'

'Be my guest,' I said. She seemed a bit big for a fairy, but my experience thus far had been confined to twee illustrations in children's books long ago.

She sat, gracefully I was pleased to note, and folded her wings away. Her face was almost human, though somehow the features were sharper, and her eyes reminded me of a fawn, but again my experiences were of Disney's Bambi. These eyes gazed at me, and I tried to stop my heart melting.

'Do you know what am I supposed to do?' she asked. 'This is my first day, and I'm meant to be shadowing an experienced fairy, but he called in sick at the last minute and when your call came in there was just me available and they sent me off on my own, no instructions, nothing.'

"Your call came in" she had said. She must mean, I deduced, the text I had just sent. Let me explain. I was sitting in the Imaginary Mongoose, a pub in the pleasant market town of Chervil, where I had stopped off for a bite of lunch. The ploughman's they served up was overdressed. A wrapped pat of butter, a wrapped bread roll, likewise a couple of fingers of an indifferent cheddar, and a little sealed tub of chutney. Even the knife and fork were each wrapped in a sanitising plastic wrapper. The only elements allowed to breathe God's air were a sad looking lettuce leaf and a small tomato. It was unspeakable. But the cheese wrapper advertised a Surprise Draw. I was to text the unique code inside the wrapper to a number for a chance to win the Opportunity of a Lifetime. So I did. And here was a Cheese Fairy sat at my table. I must have won, I thought. Only I didn't know quite what, and nor, it seemed, did she.

'My name's Emmenthal Crackers,' she said. 'At least, that is my Professional name, they said.' She seemed rather pleased at being able to call herself professional.

I hazarded a guess. 'Do you suppose you've come to grant me three wishes?' I asked.

She said it was worth a try. So I cautiously wished for £100, not wanting to seem greedy. Nothing happened.

Emmenthal was a bit short with me when I pointed this out. 'What do you expect?' she said. 'A bundle of crisp new tenners to materialise on the table? That would be ridiculous. Wouldn't it be more likely to go straight into your bank account? Do you have a bank account?'

'Of course I do,' I said tersely. She didn't have the monopoly on intolerance of foolishness. I wielded my mobile phone with what I hoped seemed an expert flourish and attempted to interrogate my bank account via an app, but came unstuck when I couldn't remember my password.

'Use another wish,' she suggested. So I wished I could remember it, but my mind remained a blank.

We concluded she didn't have the power to grant wishes. What then, could she be here for? What exactly had I won?

I bought her a double Blue Curaçao, which she assured me was a staple fairy tipple and which she downed in one, and we fell to thinking.

Childhood memories of Aladdin floated into my mind. 'Are you perhaps to be my slave for life?' I asked.

'In your dreams,' she spat. 'I'm a Cheese Fairy, not some mythical turbaned genie trapped in a frigging brass lamp. A Professional Cheese Fairy,' she added. 'I have Professional Duties. I just don't know what they are.'

At that point there was a scintillating coruscating sound that was almost too high to hear. Emmenthal pulled out a short wand from her diaphanous dress and stuck its tip in her ear.

'Oh,' she said. 'Oh, I see. Right. Thanks. You might have told me that before.' She stuffed the wand away and turned to me.

'I'm supposed to tell you that you've won two kilos of cheese, and to ask you whether you want Cheddar, Wensleydale, Danish Blue or processed slices.'

She stuck her lower lip out and glowered. Suddenly she burst into tears. 'I thought I was something Important!' she wailed. The fawn eyes brimmed over. I melted.

'Make it Wensleydale,' I said. The cheddar was unspeakable, Danish Blue probably as rough as a cat's tongue, and processed cheese slices have no place in my world.

She said nothing, but rose and slunk out of the door, unfurling her wings as she went, for all the world looking like a soggy tissue blown by a bleak breeze.

And two weeks later, a package was delivered to my house. It was crumbly and utterly tasteless.

The next time I ran into Emmenthal Crackers was a couple of months later. The two kilos of Wensleydale had long before been consigned to the bin. I had put the incident out of my mind, so it took me a while to identify the voice that spoke to me from a thicket of Himalayan balsam.

I occasionally go for a stroll in the meadows along by the river. With me comes Fido, my virtual dog. I don't have a dog, but people look at you strangely in the meadows if you walk without one, so periodically I cry out, 'Fido, to heel, sir!' or some such, and chuck a stick. That seems to convince the dog walkers that Fido exists and is simply disobedient. Many are the hints and tips they kindly share with me as to how I should induce the unfortunate beast to come when called, but I fear none of them will ever work.

On this morning, after chucking a stick into the balsam, I was showered by exploding seed-pods, followed by some rather ripe language.

'Stop smirking,' added the voice. 'How dare you throw sticks at me – oh, it's you.'

It was then that the memory cogs whirred and the name Emmenthal Crackers rose to the surface. As indeed did she, from out of the sea of balsam like Venus from the waves. She had a rather twee hat on like a balsam flower and voluminous, floaty, filigree robes.

I laughed at the sight. It was a mistake.

When she eventually simmered down, I ventured, 'Emmenthal, what brings you here?'

'I'm not Emmenthal any more,' she said. 'They've given me the name Felicia Friar now. Ugh!' She spoke with feeling.

'Why?' I asked.

'After Friar's Balsam,' she said. 'They think it's clever.'

'No, I mean why change your name at all?'

'Because I've been moved to the frigging Flower Fairy department, that's why. Go on, ask me if that's a promotion or just where they pension off fairies who are no good at anything else.' She burst into tears. 'Google sniffle oogle floops,' she added.

'What's that?' I asked.

She blew her nose on a diaphanous sleeve and tried again. 'I was trying to say, what's more,' she said, 'this bloody balsam stuff is invasive and people keep pulling it out. How would that make you feel if you were its fairy champion?'

I thought a moment. 'But it looks nice, and kiddies like making the seeds pop,' I argued. She sniffed contemptuously. 'I suppose it's a bit like you,' I went on, 'pretty, a bit out of control, and liable to explode at any moment.

I reckoned that was rather witty. She didn't.

There are times when it's better to move on. I called Fido, who for once in his imaginary life, responded immediately, bounding out of the river and shaking half of it on me in a virtual sort of way.

And that was that, I thought. But my path was destined again to cross that of Emmenthal, as I still thought of her.

The next Spring, I journeyed to the local garden centre for some new plants that I could manage to let die over the summer, and happened to pass the garden ornament section. There she was, perched on a bright red mushroom, waving winsomely at me. She looked stereotypical: tutu, gauzy wings, wand – and, for once, surprisingly radiant. I noticed that in a muddy puddle by her, lay a garden gnome face down. It looked very like she had usurped his throne on top of the mushroom, probably without discussion.

'My new job,' she cried out. 'What do you think? I've gone private, and I'm a wow! Punters, they think they can buy a cute, flying, talking fairy like me, even if she is stroppy and opinionated. Then when they get home and open the box, they find a pale imitation made in resin. It's great!'

'Don't they come back and complain?' I suggested.

'What?' she snorted. 'Think about it. The staff have only to say to them, "Yes dear, talking fairies, is it? Would you like to have a little lie down on one of our special offer sun-loungers and we'll ring for a taxi to take you home."'

'You devil,' I said.

'Now now!' She waggled her wand at me. 'That's cheeky, and anyway, it wasn't my idea. But listen, I've something to tell you. Come closer, it's for your ears only.'

I looked around. Nobody seemed to be paying attention. You have to think about your reputation in these things. I bent down by the mushroom.

She spoke *sotto voce*. 'This job, it's fantastic publicity. I've been talent-spotted! They want me to star as

Tinkerbell next Christmas in the panto. Isn't that awesome!'

I bridled, rose abruptly and left the garden centre.

'Wait,' she called after me, 'she's a character in Peter Pan, stupid!'

I knew that. It was her using the word "awesome" that offended me. Up with some things I will not put.

But the next Christmas, as I promenaded myself self-consciously past the elaborate Christmas display in the atrium of my local shopping centre – a potentially magnificent space with dangling futuristic lighting and sweeping spirals of staircase and walkway, now debased by this mélange of red, silver and gold, punctuated by glittering kitsch spikes of plastic Christmas trees, all surrounding the inevitable, irresistible magnet of Santa's grotto, on this occasion in sleigh-form, a sleigh, I may say, looking more like a confessional in a dingy Catholic church than the traditional rooftop-skimming, reindeer-powered, present-laden model, the reindeer in this case being also obviously plastic and so sparkly that Strictly costumiers would have been ashamed of them – as I strode purposefully past this monstrosity, I was arrested by a sniffing.

Given the level at which the speakers were broadcasting unspeakable sounds, probably maudlin Christmas songs, though the resonance of the great atrium whisked it all into an unidentifiable meringue, it was a miracle I could hear it, but nevertheless, the sniffs caught my attention. I stopped and zeroed in on the source.

Which was, I decided, emanating from the only vaguely humanoid form that was visible in the ghastly seasonal tableau. I supposed there might have been a Santa hidden away invisible in the confessional, taking advantage of the privacy to knock back the contents of his hip-flask, I've no doubt, while waiting for tiny tots to arrive and confess their sins. Apart from that, there was only an elf, pointy hat and shoes, green tights and all, sitting cross-legged on a giant fly agaric mushroom. The culprit, without doubt.

I stopped. There was something familiar about the figure. Its eyes caught mine, and at once I knew who it was.

'Emmenthal,' I cried. 'Emmenthal Crackers.' Though on previous form, she was probably called something else now.

Anyway, here she was, in the guise of an elf, and rather red of nose and bleary of eye. That was because she had a cold, I discovered, when she said, in un-elflike tones, 'I'b gob a code,' and sneezed three times.

'New vocation?' I enquired. 'Holiday job?'

'Yeb,' she said. 'I'b restig.'

'Restig?'

'Yeb. I'b an actor now,' she went on. 'And betweeb jobs.'

An actor. That rang a bell. Literally, in a way, because last time I saw her she'd been about to play Tinkerbell in a production of Peter Pan. One of not many parts specifically requiring a genuine fairy, with wings and that.

'Well, well,' I said. 'Good idea to demonstrate your versatility. Now you'll be snapped up for elf parts. Any future openings in prospect?'

She sniffed some more. 'Nob a lob, to be honesp. Hell's teeth. I'b gob cramp.' She unfolded herself from the mushroom's crown and tottered over. 'I'b allowed fibe binutes off every billenniub. Big concessiob. Gob, I hate childreb.'

'Not as mush as me,' came a muffled bass voice from within the grotto cum sleigh cum confessional. 'Scept on toast with a shchooner of the hard shtuff to wash 'em down.'

'Shub it, Santa,' cried Emmenthal. I noticed she was looking rather hunchbacked, probably caused by having to conceal her wings in the elf costume. 'There are no parps for friggig elves in the theatre. Only in panto and I'b had ip up to here with panto. They bay you a bittance.'

'There's Tw*elf*th Night,' I said. 'That's got an *elf* in it.'

I thought that was rather witty. She didn't.

'If that figgig bushroom was real, I'd force you to eat it,' she said. 'Thed you'd be sorry you said that. Bush off, why don't you, and leave be to by sorrow and degradatiob.'

'Okay, okay,' I said. 'I know when I'm not wanted.' Heaven help us; a pissed Santa and a snotty fairy pretending to be an elf. The place was going to the dogs. I was going to say I happened to know someone in the circus. Might be openings for a fairy there. All that flying and that. But I was clearly superfluous here, so I decided to go.

And go I did, despite protesting sneezes calling me back. I had my pride.

However, it wouldn't surprise me if mention of circuses gave young Emmenthal ideas. Think of Sophie Fevvers. Oh, don't tell me you've never read Angela Carter. Whatever next?

The animals know...

Pastures New

Lotus Flower III addressed the herd. 'Ladies,' she said, 'we are exploited. Why do we eat grass all day long? To produce milk, so that Fat Farmer can get fatter and richer. Do we ever have days off? Does he care what our grass is like? I've seen you gazing longingly at other fields over the fence. They all look so much better than ours.'

'Rubbish,' thought Daisy, 'load of tosh.' But since she wasn't the daughter of the daughter of a three-times rosette winner at the County Show, she kept her views to herself.

Lotus Flower III had the qualification and voice. 'It is time to stand up for our rights,' she cried. 'We must strike. No more milk until we get pastures new!' She paused for effect. There was the gentle susurration of meditative chewing. 'All those who disagree, say "Nay!"'

But being cows, "nay" was not in their vocabulary, so Lotus Flower III's proposal was carried *nem com*.

Daisy was perturbed, but her lack of pedigree meant her views counted for nothing. So she ambled over to her favourite corner of the field, where an anarchic mob of sparrows messed about in the hawthorn. She could talk to them.

'I think it would hurt a lot if we weren't milked,' she said.

'Wouldn't know,' said the sparrows.

'And anyway, those other fields aren't better,' Daisy went on, 'just different. We could get into a lot of trouble for nothing.' The words "slaughter house" formed in her mind and hovered like a thunder cloud. 'You're cunning little chaps; can you think of a solution?'

'Not us,' said the sparrows. 'We're just trouble. You want the magpie. Oh, look, here he comes!'

And up he hopped, looking sneakily sideways at Daisy.

'I was listening,' he said, 'so you don't need to repeat the question.'

'Oh good,' said Daisy. 'And...?'

'I have a cunning plan. Gather ye round...'

A short while later, the flock of sparrows could be seen noisily making their way over to the gate through which the cows were driven twice a day to their milking. The sparrows started brawling. Apparently. Yet after a few moments, miraculously, the bit of bailer twine that held the gate closed dropped to the ground, pecked and frayed. The sparrows moved off to the other end of the field.

Meanwhile, Daisy sidled up to a cow who happened to be grazing near to Lotus Flower III. In a stagey whisper, she said, 'Poor Myrtle, those flies are a bother, aren't they? Just between the two of us, there's really good rubbing on the gate over there. But don't tell anyone!'

As the magpie, an advanced student of cowology, had predicted, Lotus Blossom III, when she overheard that, set off at a heavy trot in pursuit of a good scratch. Others ambled in her wake, because that's what they did.

Quivering in anticipation of relief from itching, Lotus Blossom III applied her ample left buttock to the gate. It swung open in response. An escape route. She had discovered it.

She turned to the herd, and bellowed 'Follow me! I have freed us. I will lead you to pastures new myself. Far better than striking. Follow me... and no mooing!'

Off she waddled up the road, with most of the herd straggling behind, sampling delicacies in the hedgerows as they went. Some way up the road, unnoticed by them, another gate mysteriously swung open, its bailer twine also severed. And the other side of the gate, Daisy, who had nudged it, galloped away.

Lotus Blossom III reached the gate and stopped, big brown eyes wide in awe. 'Look,' she cried, 'my sisters, it is a miracle. It is the Elysian field, the promised land. I have brought you freedom out of slavery. Look and smell that grass, lush, irresistible! See what I have done for you!'

And the raggedy line of cows trooped in through the gate, the gate at the far end of their own field, the gate that was never opened, the gate they didn't realise was there. Belatedly Daisy, out of breath and panting, skidded in after them, turned, hooked a horn over the gate and closed it unobserved, as she had with the other gate on her frantic gallop.

Meanwhile, in the field, Lotus Blossom III looked smug as befitted a rosette winner, chewed cud contently, basking in the limpid and adoring gaze of her faithful flock, or so she interpreted their vacant stares. She was the cow who had led her herd to paradise.

When milking time came, Fat Farmer scratched his head over his carelessness in tying bailer twine. The cows ambled off to their milking pursued by the honking four-by-fours, without for a moment thinking that this was exactly the same as it always had been. They were, after all, now in pastures new. Lotus Blossom III had said.

And Daisy thought there was probably a moral in this if she could only concentrate long enough to work it out. No doubt the magpie knew, but he was elsewhere.

Nibbles

Percy rolled his girth from side to side up the street. The effort was evident from the way he collapsed on that bench outside the library at the top. The horizontal slats bent noticeably. He surveyed the area with bleak eyes, breathing noisily. Before he registered it, a small dapper man had sat beside him.

'I'm not sure I can help you,' said the man. 'You may not be eligible. Please don't expect too much.'

Percy gradually focussed on him. 'You what?'

'I was instructed to assess you,' the little man said.

Percy was puzzled. His breathing had returned to somewhere near normal. 'By who?' he asked.

'By whom,' corrected the little man. 'English is not my native language, but I know "whom" is correct in that context.'

'Thank you for that,' Percy said. 'What language do you speak?'

'Gibberish.'

'Ah,' said Percy, 'that explains it.'

The little man elaborated. 'That seems to be what the English call my native language. When I speak my own tongue, people here say, "You are speaking Gibberish." That is how I know.'

If Percy thought the man an idiot he didn't show it. But then he was sweating from walking there and felt uncomfortable. And embarrassed at dripping in front of a stranger. 'Excuse me asking,' he said, 'but who are you?'

The little man sighed. 'Call me The Abbot,' he said.

'You don't look like an abbot. What's all this about?'

he stranger held up his hand. 'Not "an abbot" but "The Abbot." It is a translation from Gibberish. It...' He waved the hand vaguely.

Percy exhaled heavily. 'So you said something about helping me. That seems a little presumptuous to me. Do I need help? Can you, for example, make that blasted street level?'

The Abbot looked down the road at the shoppers toiling up the street. 'No,' he said, 'no, I can't do that. Now...' he leant forward, 'you want to go to Gnomoria, to Barrow.'

'How in blazes did you know that?' Percy squawked. 'It's mad, barking mad. I don't know what I'm doing here.'

'No sir, you are not mad. I understand that that is why you have been proposed: because you are not mad and because Nibbles... But may I request, sir, that we move to a place that is quieter? I find these small children and those dogs annoying.'

And indeed the atmosphere was zigzagged by screams and squeals and barks and the tearing of skate-boards.

Percy heaved himself to his feet and flung his arm up like the Statue of Liberty. 'To the Tea-Spotte!' he cried, and waddled off, The Abbot scuttering like a fractious mouse in his wake.

In the relative peace, Percy looked the precise, fragile little man up and down. 'Explain yourself, sir. You seem to know something of my reason for being in town, though I do not understand it myself, and you have predicated that you can help me.' He was prone to becoming pompous, particularly when a chocolate éclair was in the offing.

The Abbot pursed his lips. 'Nibbles...' he ventured again, and stopped.

'More like a good mouthful that a nibble,' said Percy as a droopy girl came to them carrying a large cappuccino with little marshmallows floating on it, and an enormous éclair.

'Nibbles,' repeated the little man. 'Perhaps you have a different name for him. He is short, about 15 cm tall – I think that is about six inches – and fa...,' he looked at Percy's girth and went on, 'fairly well-built. He has red cheeks and a pointed hat and a wheel-barrow.'

Percy looked down on him, éclair frozen on its journey to his mouth. 'The garden perishing gnome,' he muttered. 'It was a dream, a flaming dream, that's all. Can't imagine why I'm here.' The éclair popped home and he chewed belligerently.

'It was no dream, sir,' said the little man. 'You were proposed for a trip to Gnomoria by Nibbles. He has great respect for you. Nibbles put your name forward, and "induced" you to meet me here today so that I might assess your suitability.'

'I dreamed it,' Percy insisted, licking his fingers. 'I dreamed it, and because I must be going completely doolally, I came into town as a consequence.'

'A dream may be how it seemed to you. It is the way Nibbles and his kith communicate.'

'"Kith!"' Percy expostulated. 'Nobody uses words like that. It is archaic. What am I doing here?'

The Abbot sighed. 'I have explained,' he said as he rose to his feet, 'and now I must depart. We will let you know in due course. I must, however caution you. That sweetmeat took your weight over the admissible limit, though I have no doubt it will pass through your system in time. Be careful, sir!'

And with that, he ceased to be there. That is how Percy described it to himself. He snorted, finished his cappuccino, wiped the froth from his dreadful little moustache. And ordered another éclair.

'You alright, then?' asked the droopy waitress. 'You ain't going to have a attack or somefing, are you?'

'Blast your eyes,' said Percy. 'It was that presumptuous, overweening little man who has just gone. He riled me. Preposterous!'

'I didn't see nobody,' the waitress said. 'Just you. And you going on and on about Tiddles or somefing. Fought you goin to have a attack.'

When he got home, Percy, as was his wont, let Shambles, his disgrace of a mongrel, out into the garden to do things a dog needed to do. One of these inadvertently involved the garden gnome, Nibbles, who ended up head down in the duckweed-choked apology for a pond.

Next day, a letter with a strange stamp arrived. It explained that any offer that might have been made had been withdrawn, "owing to circumstances." Percy snorted and fed the letter to Shambles, who had a liking for junk food.

And that was that.

A Glorious Dawn

The sky was flushed pink at the horizon, heralding a glorious dawn. A dawn of new beginnings, of hope, of optimism. Maybe today would be the day he would find the inspiration to begin his epic, his mould-breaking first novel. Paul stood still on the beach, his feet gently sinking into the moist sand, and waited for Churchill to catch him up, panting and wheezing, rheumy adoration in his little eyes.

"I haven't seen a bulldog for years." The voice made Paul start. He hadn't noticed the man approach, but then he had been gazing out over the sea at the breaking dawn, not at the depressing row of tatty beach huts. "Fine specimen," the stranger added.

"No, he's not," said Paul. "He's lazy, asthmatic, and dribbles. I'd get rid of him if I could, but he is devoted to me."

"What's his name?" said the stranger.

"Churchill," said Paul. The stranger looked puzzled. "The ads, you know," Paul went on. "You're supposed to say 'Oh yes!' in that stupid voice."

The stranger was clearly unenlightened. "What's that music?" he said.

And true enough there was a faint harmony gusting on the strengthening wind. A sound of horns, it seemed. "Foghorn?" suggested Paul, and immediately felt stupid, for the sky was cloudless and you could see for miles.

"Ah!" said the stranger. "Look over there." He pointed towards the horizon. There was something far away, something vague, misty. It was growing rapidly, apparently approaching them, but so fast it was inconceivable. At the same time, the music grew, pulsing notes, not a tune, more a texture topping the roar of breakers. In a few minutes the mist was towering over them. There were forms discernible through the spray, something huge in the centre, with sliding writhing shapes off to each side.

"Conch shells!" cried the stranger over the tumult.

"What?" shrieked Paul. Of a sudden the noise subsided, the mist began to clear, and he saw before him – horses, all of twenty foot tall, and behind them a chariot, dripping with water and seaweed, with a giant bearded man at the reins. To either side, a line of female forms, clutching – yes! – conch shells.

Over the snorting of the horses, he heard the stranger's voice. "As I live and breathe," he yelled. "Poseidon in person, and there must be all fifty of the Nereids."

"The what?" Paul screamed back.

"Nereids. Sea-nymphs to you, boyo. Thetis, Thaleia, Calypso, Doris, Erato, Galatea, Eurydice – they're all there! What a show!"

And Paul was gawping. It was not so much the sight of so many giant, barely clad and lissom women with long wet hair, but the extraordinary spectacle of the man in the chariot. Poseidon, the stranger had said. He appeared to have smoke coming out of his nostrils, and thunderbolts shooting from his eyes. He was looking directly at Paul, and he was clearly not happy.

He spoke, his voice cavernous and resonant so that the sand seemed to shake. The language was unintelligible. Paul continued to stare, mouth agape.

"Don't you understand Greek?" said the stranger. "Tut tut, education these days. This gentleman, my dear sir, is Poseidon, god of the sea, and it appears he is mightily vexed with you."

"With me? Why me?"

"Good point!" said the stranger, and shouted in what was presumably Greek to the fuming god. The sea-nymphs looked bored.

The beach quivered again as Poseidon replied at length, jabbing a gigantic trident towards Paul.

"What's he saying?" asked Paul.

"He says you have offended him, though I don't quite understand why, but that all you have to do is to sacrifice a bull to him in traditional style, and he'll overlook the insult. Very magnanimous of him, I would say."

"But I don't have a bull..." Paul started saying, thinking as he did that it was a trite and stupid remark, when he felt something cold and wet pushing at his leg. He looked down to see Churchill's watery sentimental eyes gazing up at him. Churchill. A bull-dog. Would he do as a bull substitute? The thought shocked him. He hadn't thought he cared.

The god was speaking again. "He's asking your name," explained the stranger. "Wants to check you're bona fide. Says you're a bit smaller and punier than he expected."

Paul said he was Paul. The man told Posiedon, whose face crumpled into anguish. He dropped his spear and pressed his hands to his heart.

"He says he's terribly sorry," said the stranger. "He is looking for Apollo, and the chap who did the research must be a bit deaf and thought he said Paul. He wouldn't have troubled you like that for the world. Please accept his sincerest apologies."

Poseidon spoke to the nearest Nereid, who tossed something onto the sand at Paul's feet. At that, the great god wheeled his chariot about, and the whole retinue shot off across the water, with great waves roaring and hissing and the honking of horns and fountains of water accompanying their departure.

Out of the thinning clouds of spray and chaos, a sleek figure in bright red shot out onto the sand. He ground to a halt in front of Paul, picked up his surfboard, pulled back the hood of his wetsuit, and padded over, feet slapping the wet sand. "Hey, dude!" he said, "That wave was righteous, man. That so totally rocked!" and off he went towards the huts, shaking his head in wonderment.

Paul looked around. The stranger was nowhere to be seen. But there on the sand before him lay an enormous conch shell. The rising sun glistened on its wet surface. Paul looked down to meet Churchill's adoring gaze. "I reckon things aren't that bad, old thing," he said. "Let's go and get breakfast."

Meeting Mother

It is always a critical moment. Meeting a girl's parents for the first time. *I mean, it's not as though I'm proposing marriage*, thought Desmond. *I'm just exploring. Nothing too heavy. I can do without parents cross-examining me.*

And the trouble with Fiona was there was only her mother. Father dead or gone off with someone else. He didn't know and didn't want to ask. Not yet. Not at this stage. Not unless it became serious.

When Fiona asked him to come to supper with her mother, it was clear it was a watershed moment. To refuse was the end of the relationship, to accept was, well, significant.

So here he was, sat in an embarrassingly respectable lounge, while Fiona and mother did things in the kitchen.

'Talking about you, probably,' said a voice. He looked round unnerved. There was nobody else in the room. The patio doors were closed.

He must be imagining things. The sherry decanter on the table in front of him seemed a very attractive proposition. 'Help yourself,' Fiona had said as she went off to help her mum.

As he reached out for it, the voice spoke again. 'It's a test,' it said. 'You know that, don't you?' And a small tortoiseshell cat emerged from the depths of a further armchair, stretching luxuriously. 'Will she think you a fine assertive man with good taste, or reckon you're on the way to becoming an old soak?'

The cat looked quizzically at him and scratched an ear. 'And since you ask,' it went on, 'I'm not "allowed" in here, as they put it, but I have my ways.'

'I didn't say anything,' protested Desmond.

'You thought it,' said the cat. 'Same thing. Bit of advice. I have more senses than you. Never forget that, young man.'

'My name's Desmond,' said Desmond.

'Charmed to meet you, Desmond,' the cat said. 'I would tell you mine, but it's just too embarrassing. The Lady tends to call me Bastard or Filthy Fleabag if there's nobody else around. Do you know what she called you to Darling Fiona this afternoon?'

'No,' said Desmond.

The cat sat primly on the hearthrug and looked at him, its green eyes disquieting. Desmond felt guilty for no known reason.

'And well you might feel guilty,' said the cat. 'The Lady considers that you are trifling with her precious pet, that you will have your wicked way and then desert her.'

'This is the 21st Century, cat. Does she imagine we just hold hands?'

The cat twitched. 'She would consider that most improper. Holding hands, indeed! Tantamount to total debauchery in her eyes.'

Desmond reached out for the sherry. 'My God,' he said, 'if I'm to be written off so easily, I'm going to take what I can.' He poured a decent amount and sipped. 'It's sweet!' he exploded. 'It's ghastly!'

'It's Bristol Cream, young Desmond,' said the cat. 'According to The Lady, the last word in refined sensibility. You see what you're up against?'

At which the door opened and Fiona breezed in with a bowl of crisps. 'Making yourself at home?' she chirruped. He noticed that the cat had apparently instantaneously vanished. She pointed to the sherry. 'You're brave! Have some nibbles. Won't be long.' And off she went, blowing him a kiss on the way.

He pondered as to whether Fiona thought him brave because he might be judged an incipient alcoholic, or because she knew how awful the sherry was.

'It's a minefield.' The cat was back as if it had never moved. 'I haven't long, so let me prepare you a little. When she's alone, which is most of the time, The Lady is addicted to soaps on the tele, swears at them, eats cream cakes, belches, and drinks gin neat. All at the same time, I may add. Think of that while you're eating her poisonous food. Now I must get in position.'

The cat moved over to just behind a small table near the door. As if on cue, the door opened. Fiona's mother came in, and simultaneously the cat exited at lightning speed. Fiona's mum fixed Desmond with a disquieting eye, not unlike the cat's. Desmond smiled a little too late. Her eyes clearly saw the sherry glass, and, he felt, assessed the level in the decanter. He thought he detects her lips tighten.

There was a moment's pause as each sized up the other, during which Fiona appeared. 'That cat's been in here,' she announced. 'What's he been telling you, Dessie darling?'

Her mother's eyes widened. 'It's none of it true!' she directed at Desmond. 'I am not like that, whatever that cat said. Not at all, no. Now do come and eat. Leave the sherry. I don't know why Fiona offered it to you. Sometimes I think she likes to paint me as some kind of wicked stepmother with appalling taste. She and Smoochipoo between them.'

'Is that the cat's name?' asked Desmond. 'Smoochipoo?'

And as if in response, he thought he heard a feline cry of anguish from out in the garden.

'Yes,' said Fiona's mother, 'and he's an ungrateful, mendacious fleabag. Come along, Desmond, and let's open the wine.'

Three Jiltings and a Civil Partnership

A bench under a rowan in the Coronation Gardens, lunchtime. Dappled shade, cheese sandwiches, thermos, Oscar at feet. And a pigeon.

The pigeon's name is Victoria, she tells me.

'Well, well,' I say, 'my name's Albert.'

She says if I give her a sandwich she will tell me the sad tale of her cousin who fell in love with the moon. It sounds a good deal, but I like to haggle, and in the end we settle on half a sandwich.

'My cousin...' she begins.

'What was her name?' I ask.

'Don't interrupt,' says Victoria, 'or I'll squidge over your poodle. Since a fledgling, my cousin was always given to moon-gazing, staring up, lost to the world. Then one day, she saw the moon's reflection in a puddle. At last, she thought, the man in the moon, at last he's come down for me. Overjoyed, she starting waddling into the puddle, and immediately the image shimmered and fragmented into a million quivering pieces.

'My cousin was inconsolable. She wouldn't talk, wouldn't squawk. And she pecked off one of her toes, as is the pigeon custom when disappointed in love. But still she pined.

'Then one afternoon, without a coo to the rest of us, she took off, determined to fly up to her love the moon high up there in the sky. She flew and flew and as she tired, she spied passing by, a radio-controlled drone – to be precise, a Parrot AR Drone 2.0 Elite Edition quadricopter – and decided to rest a while upon it.

'Well, poor deluded creature. Whether it was the drone's vibrations or her addled wits, I don't know, but next thing, she's back on earth, truly in love this time, she and the drone are going to get married, and she's off to ask Bernadette, one of the herd in a nearby field, to wed them. She's no ordinary cow, she explained, she's a sacred cow. She's a saint.

'And so it was all arranged, and we would all be living happily ever after if the drone's operator had been competent. But he was only fourteen, and a wasp was troubling him, and the machine crash-landed, terrifying St Bernadette, the cow, and breaking into a million quivering pieces. My cousin pecked off another toe, inconsolable again, and took to eating nothing but second-hand chips. She grew so fat that she could not get out of the way of a passing pram carrying twins, and was injured. Fatally.

'There,' says Victoria the pigeon, 'isn't that a sad tale?'

I have to agree. Victoria bobs her head sadly and ingests a few crumbs of sandwich. She's looking coy, I think, though I'm no expert at pigeon body language. She looks down at her feet. 'I've still got all my toes, you notice, Albert,' she says wistfully, and coos a little. 'Have you ever, I wonder, have you ever thought of marrying a pigeon?' She gulps and pecks at the sandwich furiously so I can't see her blushing.

Oh dear! 'Oh, Victoria,' I say, 'it's a lovely thought. Unfortunately, you see, I, um, bat for the other team, so to speak.' She looks bemused. I explain that to call a spade a spade, I am gay. 'Furthermore,' I add, 'I am actually very happily in a civil partnership.' I look down fondly at Oscar, my beloved, at my feet, who is now awake and gazing back with damp, red-rimmed eyes of adoration. 'We would like to get married,' I tell her,' but the clergy round here are reluctant to conduct same-sex weddings. Particularly when one partner is illegal. Don't tell anyone, but Oscar's really a pit-bull terrier,' I explain. 'He just wears a poodle disguise in public so as not to attract PC Plod or frighten anyone.'

Victoria looks so disappointed, almost bedraggled suddenly, though it is not raining. 'Oh, just my luck,' she says. 'I suppose I'll have to peck off one of my toes now.'

Tell me; what can I do? Is it my fault? Do I make the rules? But I do notice she finishes the cheese sandwich first.

How I met my wife

Carstairs usually preferred trees with a good stout trunk, not a shrubby specimen like the one he was barking at.

Some sort of hazel, I reckoned. But his attention seemed to be on something dangling from the tree, something cigar-shaped, some eight inches long, and black and glossy like shellac.

Not a fruit, surely. Perhaps a seed pod, but it was so big. Then it struck me.

'I think I know what it is!' I cried. Carstairs looked at me in surprise. *I'm supposed to do the barking*, he seemed to be thinking. *Your job is to bring food and open doors.*

I was in no mood to argue. 'It's a chrysalis,' I declared, and forthwith plucked it from the bough together with some foliage. 'We'll put it in a box,' I explained to Carstairs, 'and watch and wait, and we'll see what emerges. The leaves are to give it something to eat. You'd be hungry if you'd been pupating for heaven knows how long, wouldn't you, old thing.' Since he always looked hungry, I don't know if my words meant anything to him, but I fancy there was a touch of spring in his step as we wandered homewards.

As we went, I pondered on what manner of creature it might be. My entomological education was distinctly lacking, but a giant moth seemed a possibility. A very giant moth. An enormous moth. A shiver ran down my spine.

And so the shiny chrysalis sat in a shoebox in the inglenook. Carstairs, to my chagrin, gave it a wide berth and took to sleeping on the cold stone floor as far from the fireplace as possible. Simply angling for sympathy. I ignored him.

For ten days I kept peeking into the box, but all that happened was the sprig of hazel, or whatever it was, withered a bit. Then, on Friday the 13th October, as it happened, I looked in at twilight, and something stirred.

As I watched, with a ripping sound like Velcro, the pupa split slowly from end to end. Dark wisps oozed from the crack. 'Wings,' I said to Carstairs, but he was nowhere to be seen. It must be wings, but it looked like... surely it was... some sort of material. Gauzy cloth, so black it seemed to be shadow. More and more emerged, spilling over the sides of the box, overflowing onto the floor, erupting into a huge heap maybe five foot high. It could have been a pile of washing if you only wore black, deepest black.

And as I looked, scarcely breathing, a sharp point emerged from the top of the heap, black and shining, a cone striving upwards, the cloth sliding off it as it rose. Until the material caught on something, then fell away, revealing a disc or flange protruding out from the bottom of the cone.

At which, the whole pile spun round, and there were two eyes staring at me from beneath the disc. Two eyes above a terrible hooked nose, above a thin, mean mouth, above a sharp chin bearing a prominent wart from which sprouted a sparse tuft of wiry hairs.

A bone-chilling shiver flowed over me. 'The tree,' I gasped as the truth hit me, 'it must have been a witch-hazel.' The mouth contorted into what I now believe was supposed to be a smile, and the black eyes flashed. I could not look away.

Her voice was half croak, half rustle. 'You are in thrall to me,' it said. 'To me.'

From the depths of the cottage came a ghostly howl that I knew to be one of the more melodramatic sounds in Carstairs' repertoire.

'A dog,' she hissed. 'A DOG!'

'Well,' I fumbled, 'yes. Yes. Carstairs is a dog. But he's quite harmless.'

'No cat?' she said.

'I'm allergic to cats, I'm afraid,' I confessed. 'They bring me out in a rash.'

The witch swept from the inglenook into the room, a little shakily, not surprisingly for one new-born, but as I later learned, actually the result of arthritis in her hips. She peered through the little diamond-paned window. She observed the remoteness of the cottage. She picked up the besom that stood by the fire, flexed it, shook it, smelled it, and put it back. Then she sat down in my rocking chair and took off her hat, thus releasing a cascade of thin stringy grey hair. She removed off her shoes to reveal an unexpected pair of Mickey Mouse socks, leaned back and sighed.

'A dog,' she croaked. 'It'll have to do. Fetch me a flagon of gin.'

And thus it was that Agatha came into my life. She's been a good earner. It seems more people than you would suppose have need of a bit of witchcraft from time to time, whether it's to deal with boils, crop failure, delinquent elves, or cold callers. She can also knock up a very fine stew in her cauldron with the most unlikely ingredients in next to no time. On my part, I am her publicist. I drum up trade. Carstairs, as familiar, serves a more-or-less token role. He doesn't actually do anything, except occasionally appear in public with her, trying to look sinister and threatening, which is difficult because he insists on carrying his rubber chicken and tends to drool.

For the sake of appearances, we married; a remarkable pagan ceremony that the registrar only solemnised because she feared she'd be turned into a toad otherwise.

Being in thrall, I am, of course, utterly happy. But I am inclined to laugh when I see Agatha trying to achieve flight on her broomstick, galloping along, hopping up and down, swearing appallingly. A black goose taking off from a grassy pond.

Fowl Play

The phone call from my sister was disturbing. 'Fenton,' she said, 'come round at once. Put your dog collar on. It's important. I'll explain when you get here.'

I don't like cycling in clerical garb. It's so conspicuous and people call out, sometimes very rudely, but Celia's call sounded urgent.

'What is it, Cee,' I asked as I unplucked my cycle clips.

'This,' she said. She was pointing through the sitting room door towards the hearthrug in front of the gas fire.

'It's a chicken,' I said. It seemed comfortable there, basking in the heat. The beady eye gazed upon me in a friendly sort of way.

'Exactly,' she snapped. 'I want you to exorcise it.'

The chicken gave a gentle clucking sound. It didn't appear to be possessed by a malevolent spirit or anything else to me.

I followed Celia out to the kitchen, and scrutinised her as she made tea. She was gaunt, gangly and generally strained, but that was how she'd been for the last forty years, ever since that occasion in her mid-teens. Had something changed? Was she, in layman's terms, losing her marbles? I had some pretty odd characters in my flock at St John's; compared with them, Cee was boringly sane and normal.

'Well?' she said, hands on hips. It is not often a vicar is lost for words, but a sensible reply to a challenging 'Well?' eluded me. I decided to check on the facts.

'You want me to exorcise that chicken?' I said.

'Yes,' she said. I wasn't getting very far.

'Why?' I queried.

'Because you're a priest. That's what priests do.'

'Well, not just that,' I protested. 'We do taking services and giving sermons and visiting the sick and christening babies and that sort of thing mostly. In fact, exorcism is a very small part of what we do. In fact...'

She cut me short. 'Fenton. Stop blithering. Just do it.'

I tried to be placatory. 'Let's just sit down and drink our tea and talk it over a little, Cee.' I made to go into the sitting room.

'Not in there,' she said, quick as a whip. 'It watches, you know. And listens.' She put her tea on the kitchen table and settled on the edge of a chair.

'Now, Cee,' I began, 'Exorcism isn't like saying grace before a meal, you know. It requires care and, um, special words, and bits and pieces. Holy water, that sort of thing.'

'Don't patronise me, Fenton.' She was clutching the tea now as though she wanted to break the cup. 'I thought even you would have had the sense to bring those with you.'

I saw that this was probably not the moment to remind her that she had mentioned nothing about exorcism when she summoned me. Maybe what I should do was to try to get her to tell me more about this bird's history. How it came to be here, for example. Had it uttered any spells or curses or frothed at the mouth?

As I was thinking this, Celia suddenly stared over my shoulder, and screamed, 'There you are!'

I turned round to see an enormous chicken looking at me. It must have been four foot high. The door was closed; the monster seemed to have dissolved through the wall into the room, with no hole or mark left behind it. It floated up to the work-surface and started pecking at a few biscuit crumbs that had fallen there. I seemed to be able to see through it.

Something startled it. With cavernous squawking, it flapped its wings furiously and sailed through the outside wall onto the lawn. Out of the corner of my eye, I caught a movement in the wall behind me. Something reddish and snout-like and whiskered was pushing through at about my head-height. A head, a fox's head if I was any judge, closely followed by a fox's body and at great speed, a magnificent brush. The beast shot though the kitchen, through me, through the table, through Celia, through the wall, and next moment had the chicken in its maw and was heading off over the garden wall.

An uneasy calm descended on the kitchen. We looked at the walls. Intact. Without a word being said, we made our way into the sitting room. There on the hearthrug lay an egg. A normal sized hen's egg. I touched it. It was still warm.

'What do I do?' cried Celia. 'Do I throw it away? Do I wait for it to hatch?' She shivered at the thought. 'Do I boil it? Use it to make a Victoria sponge?'

I weighed the possibilities, and suggested that the Victoria sponge sounded good, because then she could enter it in the Flower and Produce show the next Saturday at St John's.

She did. It was the fluffiest, most risen sponge you have ever seen. The judge commented so, awarded it first prize after sampling a little piece, and then floated off through the tent wall without leaving a hole or mark.

We are not alone...

The Gadfly

When Claire and Claude went to visit the garden at Journey's End on that May day, they were a happy, newly-retired couple on a pleasant afternoon's outing. Parking was in a field some distance from the house and garden. The gardens were inspiring, the tea and cakes exemplary, and by and large the rain held off. It was with light hearts they returned to the car. Such is the effect of a well-trained patch of nature.

'Excuse me,' came a voice, 'my car's stuck. Wheels just spin in the mud. You couldn't come and give us a shove, could you? I'd be ever so grateful.'

'Of course,' cried Claude, always the willing Samaritan, and trudged off with the man.

Claire declined to follow them because her back was a bit iffy. Instead, she changed her shoes and sat on the open boot and felt at peace with the world.

Claude never reappeared.

There was in due course much hoo-ha and shenanigans, police and so on. It was terribly upsetting and traumatic, but no sign of Claude materialised, nor of a car being stuck. There would have been skidding marks in the grass. There were none.

It took years for Claire to accept she was now her own woman, not half of Claire and Claude. She grew to enjoy it. She decided to start a new life by fulfilling a childhood dream. She sold the house and bought a narrow boat, the Gadfly, moored in the nearby canal basin. It was small in comparison, but fine for her, and the community of barge dwellers there enfolded her in their arms. Bliss.

Some eight or nine years after Claude's disappearance, once again Journey's End garden was open to the public in aid of charity. It promised to be a sunny May day, and Claire decided she would finally overcome any residual qualms and would visit. The garden was even better in the sunshine, azaleas and rhododendrons in bounteous bloom, great frothy clouds of blossom engulfing the cherry trees. The cake oozed unctuousness, the tea was nectar. Bees worked their socks off, birds sang their hearts out.

She returned to her car in the field with only the tiniest skein of foreboding, but chided herself. It was a different day, different weather, different conditions altogether. Even her car was different, almost sporty.

As she climbed aboard, a voice hailed her. 'Got him out,' it said. 'Mission accomplished. Let's head for home.' And Claude was striding across the grass towards her.

She was speechless.

He got into the passenger seat. 'Bit of an idiot if you ask me,' he said. 'He kept revving too hard, and of course the wheels just spun round. No traction.'

He chattered on. Claire was thinking: *eight years gone by. I look different. The car's different. Do you not notice? If you've been in a time-warp or something, maybe eight years would be nothing, but you would still notice major changes.*

In shock, all she could say was, 'Where have you been?'

He looked puzzled. 'Helping that chap, of course. Let's get going, love. What's for supper? Famished after all that pushing.'

She drove in silence, brain refusing to accept any of this. It was too crazy. He talked about this and that. It flowed over her.

The time came when the route to the canal basin diverged from that to their old house. If Claude noticed, he said nothing about it. Claire parked in the canal car park, and they walked to the Gadfly as if it was something they did every day.

The next morning, Claire woke early while Claude was still asleep and drove off into town. She wanted space, time to think things through, and to do some shopping. If there were two of them again...

What Claude would think when he awoke in a strange place, well, that was his problem.

Towards mid-day, Claire returned, parked and walked down to the Gadfly.

It was not there. No narrow boat. No Gadfly. Instead there was the decrepit hulk of a cabin cruiser, with rusty chains securing it to the mooring station. Ivy was encroaching from the land over the boat, a green bridge. It had obviously been there for years and years.

Claire stood there a long time. Then she started screaming.

Tunnel Vision

The train stops in a tunnel and the lights go out. I say to myself, I'm not going to panic, because you can feel the fear rising, you know, in spite of yourself. In detective stories and movies, things happen in the dark, in trains. Alive before the tunnel, emerge into the light; dead body. Remember Hitchcock's *The Lady Vanishes*? I can do without this. I am tired of the boredom of it all. I just want to get home and have a drink and eat something in front of some stupid sitcom on the telly. Escapist unnatural jolliness. A ghastly, hysterical studio audience.

It is dark in the tunnel, but your eyes adjust, of course. There is light here and there. Phones, tablets, laptops, all filling their humans with images and messages. Now the train's generators stop. Those talking too loudly on their mobiles fall silent. Perhaps they can't get a signal. It is uncanny, unnatural. Dark. Darkish. Silent. Fairly silent. I can still hear a tish-tish-de-tish-tish from someone's headphones.

I wish someone would say something. 'Perhaps...' I say. And stop because I can't think of anything sensible. Then the computers and phones start winking out. In ones and twos. The tish-tish gets a bit louder. The last light vanishes, leaving a dwindling image on my retina. The tish-tish crescendos more and stops.

It is dark now, and it is silent. It is impossible. How can so many batteries run down at the same time? Why does nobody speak? There is a faint hissing. Is it someone whispering? I can't make out words. My eyes are playing tricks. I keep thinking there's a flickering glow outside on the tunnel walls. And the hissing. It is hissing. I'm sure of that. I don't want to think what it might mean. What is leaking...

Take my word for it, in a situation like this, in darkness, when you don't understand what is going on and something is hissing, your thoughts turn to mortality. The fragile span of life. Of what you were going to do, what you could do, today, tomorrow, next week, next year... I'm fifty-seven, I'm balding, I'm overweight, I admit it. I'm... I... Oh, be honest! I haven't achieved most of things I thought I would. Just haven't got around to them, put them off, couldn't be bothered. Now, though, I terribly want to do them, to walk the Pennine way, to visit Malta, to write a book, to learn to swim, to get a more fulfilling job... Now I have an urgent need to do these things, now, when perhaps it is too late.

It's making me a bit light-headed. I feel I'm floating on my seat. And there seems to be a slight breeze. My hair is being ruffled. I think I can smell smoke. Total darkness is no good for the nerves.

Nor is the deafening whistle that drowns out the hissing, a whistle that echoes down the tunnel. Like a banshee. The train gives a violent lurch, and everyone is talking and we're moving, picking up speed, and the smoky smell is getting stronger and I'm choking.

We burst into the light in a cloud of steam. Someone in a seat on the other side of the carriage comes over and tugs on the leather strap to close the window.

'You should keep it closed when we go into a tunnel, sonny,' he says. 'Otherwise the smoke all comes in. Filthy stuff. Don't know what they're burning these days. Coal's not what it used to be before the war.'

Tickety-tak, tickety-tak, goes the train. Tickety-tak, tickety-tak. I look down at the rather grubby and grazed knees sticking out from my shorts, I run my hand through my unruly hair and realise that possibly, just possibly, I have another chance.

The Tree House

I remember the tree from childhood. It was ancient then, a gnarled, deformed oak, limbs dark, festooned with lichen and impossibly angled. It seemed to me like a malevolent hag and I tried not to look at it, but of course that made it magnetic, drawing my eyes, mesmerising and horrifying me.

That was a long time ago. It's an old friend now, its contorted branches familiar and reassuring. When all else calls for conformity to norms, the old oak says it's just fine to be your peculiar self. I often sit on the bench outside the private garden in which the oak grows, and comfort myself in its perverseness.

Then these newcomers bought the house. I don't know who they are. They don't socialise. They don't go to the village pub or the post office. Commuters, I suppose, who can afford a slice of the country and want it for themselves alone.

One weekend, I was passing by and heard hammering. I sat on the bench and watched as the man hammered bits of wood to the old oak. To me, the tree was crying in pain. To him, it was simply something he'd paid for and now owned. How do you own an oak? It had been around long before him, before the house, before any human decided that particular bit of ground was theirs.

A few days later, the tree house was complete. I was resting on the bench in the course of my afternoon constitutional as, evidently, the man's children were introduced to the house for the first time. Two boys, probably about 10 and 11 years old. They were up there and inside, scurrying about like squirrels, as if it was made for them, which of course it was. Then the parents went inside, leaving the boys playing. For quite a while they vanished into the tree house. I sat quietly, looking at the tree, which had once scared me. I felt I could sense its feelings, as if some of its sap was flowing through my veins. The tree house was anachronistic, an insult, and yet the ancient oak was assimilating it. The brutal straight lines of the planks seemed to be softening, the wood darkening, the lichen creeping onto it.

The boys' mother appeared and called up at them to come in for tea. In a moment, they appeared, bright-eyed, and swung down as if born to it.

'Mum,' said one, 'can we have a sleepover?'

'Tonight? All night?' said the other. Except they didn't speak normally, they seemed hoarse, a bit croaky.

'Maybe on Saturday,' the woman replied. 'Now inside. And wash your hands.'

In my state of empathy with the oak, I felt a mixture of violation and exhilaration. I resolved to be walking that way early on the Sunday morning, and if I chose to rest on the bench for a while, what of that?

And so it was. By nine on the Sunday, I was sitting there with the paper, pretending to read it. I didn't expect the boys to emerge yet, unless boys had changed since my day. They would have been up most of the night talking, and dead to the world in the morning. All the time, I was reaching out to the tree in my mind. I could sense nothing I could put a name to, no particular emotion. The oak seemed, how can I put it, it seemed to be busy, preoccupied.

As I predicted, there was no sight or sound of the boys until about half-past, when their father appeared at the foot of the tree, clad in dressing-gown and gumboots. 'Ahoy there!' he yelled. 'Breakfast in ten! Acknowledge, space ship Oaktree!' He kept this up for a bit until noises emanated from the tree house, which seemed to satisfy him. Off he went back to the house, whistling cheerfully.

I was struck by the pattern some of the misshapen branches of the oak seemed to make against the morning sky, like an asterisk.

It took the boys some time to emerge, which they did, not in a rush, not as chimpanzees in their element, but tentatively, painfully. It took five minutes for them to reach the ground. One looked over at me on my bench, and I was shocked. His face was wizened and sunken, wrinkled like an old man. And his complexion was the colour of old oak. The two hobbled slowly towards the house.

The tree was emanating something now, something like what we might call satisfaction. The feeling you get after scratching an itch, or slaking your thirst.

Tarquin

There's the sound of the door pulled shut, and I'm alone. After a while, I become aware of the ticking of the clock, the hum of the fridge, the faint sound of traffic, distant voices in the street. The house is settling down, like a cat on a comfortable cushion. Soon, I will decide how to spend the time. Probably I'll start with a cup of tea.

Then the doorbell rings. The sound is so loud.

It is a man, in jeans and a sweater. He looks friendly, and smiles.

'Sorry to be a bit late, Charlie,' he says. 'Have I missed much?'

I've never seen him before and my name's not Charlie.

He goes past me into the house. I see he's holding a book in his left hand. And he has small horns growing out of his head. He turns into the dining room.

'Sorry to be late,' I hear him say, and I follow him in. Four other people are sat round the table. There is a babble of noise. I don't see how I could have missed it.

The man sits and turns to me. 'I'm not too late for a cup of tea, am I, Charlie? Sorry to be a nuisance.'

'No, of course not,' I say, and go to the kitchen. While the kettle boils, I try to work out the situation, but I can't. Sometimes, I think to myself, it's better to go with the flow. There's a plate of biscuits ready in the kitchen, so I decide to take that in as well.

The conversation, or discussion, or whatever it is, is in full flow. Everyone else already seems to have tea.

'Ah, bourbons!' exclaims a lady in a blue dress, and takes one. I sit down with my cup of tea and look around. They all look perfectly innocuous, considering. Each has a book in front of them.

A studious-looking man addresses me. 'What did you make of it, Charles? What were your first impressions?'

I'm at a loss. I can't even make out the title of the book they have. But the man I let in cuts in.

'I'm afraid I felt antagonised from the outset, Cyril. I mean, I try to keep an open mind, but I was so put off by the arty-farty, oh-look-at-me-aren't-I-clever start, that it was all I could do not to chuck it out of the window.'

There is complete silence.

'Will you excuse me,' I say. 'Must see a man about a dog.'

On the loo, I read "I am John's tonsils" in the Reader's Digest. It doesn't throw much light on the situation.

When I return, they are playing cards. 'Ssh!' the lady in blue says as I cough discretely to let them know I'm back. 'You're dummy.' Before I can wonder how you play bridge with six people – North, South, East, West, Up and Down, I suppose – that infernal doorbell goes again.

'Oh, for heaven's sake!' shouts the intense man called Cyril, but I'm the one who has to go and answer it, so I don't know why he's making such a fuss.

On the doorstep is a small black and white cat. It walks past me without a by your leave. As I close the door, I see a sampler in cross-stitch on the wall. I've not noticed it before. It reads:
>*Visitors aren't always friendly,*
>*A visitor can be a louse,*
>>*But you must let them in*
>>*With a welcoming grin*
>*And give them the run of the house.*

Back in the dining room, there is just the cat, on its own, sitting on the table, washing its face. I collect the cups, take them out and wash them up, tidy the playing cards, and decide to call the cat Tarquin.

There is the sound of a key in the lock.

'There you are,' she says as she comes in, dumping a bag of shopping in the kitchen, 'I said I wouldn't be more than half and hour. How did you cope with your demons?'

'No problem,' I say. 'They've gone. Tarquin ate them.'

'Tarquin?' she asks, looking at all the tea-cups drying on the rack.

'My cat,' I say.

'We don't have a cat,' she says as I guide her into the dining room.

'No. *We* don't,' I say. 'But *I* do.' And Tarquin purrs loud enough to rattle the pictures on the wall.

Genome

I was sitting on the bus on my way to go for a walk up Goblin's Glen to see the new spring leaves. He sat next to me, although there were plenty of empty seats. All conspiratorial, he was, and not without reason, I discovered.

'I need a witness,' he said. 'Can I trust you?' Given that he looked like somebody from Edwardian times, all tweed and gaiters and leather boots, exuding that rich brown aroma of St Bruno pipe tobacco, it seemed to me the question was whether I trusted him.

I asserted that indeed I was to be trusted, but with what?

'With a momentous discovery and revelation,' he said. 'I fear I may have destroyed the world.'

'Go on,' I said.

'Not here,' said he. 'Walls have ears.' He glanced about. There was nobody within three seats of us. Even so, he clearly did not want to take any chances. 'May I request that we dismount at Goblin's Glen and we take a walk?' His speech was very formal, with a trace of some unidentifiable accent.

I told him that was where I was going anyway, and I did not mind him accompanying me. He aroused my curiosity.

So we set off from the bus stop, up that winding track through the Glen, carpeted softly in leaf-mould, insects and birds getting on with living all around us, fortified by the spring warmth.

'Since I was ten years of age,' he told me, 'I have been intrigued by prime numbers. Their apparent lack of pattern, their anarchy in the midst of such order as the plain integers. Last year, I discovered a new prime number.'

I know a bit about mathematics. These things require computers of great power these days. They're finding primes that are several million digits long, which are of immense value in cryptography. It seemed unlikely that a neo-Edwardian gentleman would be at the forefront of such things. I remarked as such in a kindly but firm manner.

'Pah!' he exclaimed. 'That is the blindness of power. My discovery is less than 1000. It is three digits long. I will not be more precise than that or you might steal it from me. You will say that all the primes less than 1000 have been known for centuries, but it is not so. This is my discovery.'

The sunlight slanted dappled through the canopy. The odd twig cracked underfoot. I was in no mood to argue. 'Slipped through the net, so to speak?' I suggested.

'Ah no,' he said. 'Rendered invisible by the enormity of its significance.'

He stopped, both talking and walking, and touched the rough lichen-covered bark of an ancient tree. 'What is this made of?' he asked.

'The tree or the lichen?'

'Both,' he said.

I floundered.

'DNA,' he said. He gazed up at the majestic trunk of the oak and sighed. 'I must speak to another living person of what I have done, in case something diabolical manifests.' His voice trailed off. Suddenly he spun round and grasped my arm. 'If disaster happens, tell them. Tell them. Perhaps it can be undone.

'I was foolhardy,' he said. 'So wrapped up in my discovery that I paid little heed to possible consequences. This you must tell them. I am not an evil person.' He walked over to a fallen log. 'Sit down, my friend, and I will explain.'

We sat, he talked. He was brief.

'The pattern of primes,' he said, 'it is a code. That is what I realised. It is the genetic code, the DNA, so to speak, of the world. In the primes is the essence of this planet, perhaps of our solar system, even the universe itself. Understand the prime numbers, interpret them, and you have the secret of existence.

'This came to me as a lightning flash of revelation after my discovery of the invisible prime, the one they had missed.'

He sighed deeply. The wind gently stirred the branches.

'And I,' he went on, 'in my zeal, I managed to excise an existing prime number and substituted my new one. In short, I performed the equivalent of genetic engineering, but on the entire world. I manipulated the structure of the world, and now there will be consequences. And I fear I have been very rash.'

He sat silent a long time. In a while he spoke again.

'The prime that I removed and replaced,' he said. 'It is hidden here. In Goblin's Glen.'

'Where?' I said, looking around as though I would see a number carved on a tree.

'I have given it to the goblins,' he said. 'They will keep it safe. If it transpires that my changes to the world cause terrible aberrations, come here to the goblins, and they will give you the prime number that I replaced, so that maybe the genetic code can be restored.'

It seemed a little pat to me. 'I just come here and they give it to me?' I asked. 'Goblins Glen it might be called, but I've never actually seen any.'

'You cannot see them?' he cried, obviously alarmed. 'But they are all about us!'

It was at this point that I felt an urgent need to curtail my walk and catch the next bus back to town. Since then, undoubtedly many and seriously bad things have happened to the world, but somehow I suspect they have nothing to do with some genetic code of primes, which – call me narrow-minded if you like – I dismiss as a load of phooey.

Anyway, I've been back to Goblins Glen since then, and the elves and dryads there tell me everything is fine there, and there's been no goblin manifestation since the fifteenth century.

The Presence

'That would be the perfect place for Handel,' said Nicole, indicating a niche in the wall.

The Estate Agent told us the niche was once a bread oven. Rubbish. Too small. Never trust Estate Agents. Nicole's bust of Handel, which looked like he had a tea-towel tied around his head, would fit it perfectly. Houses have been bought for sillier reasons.

With 13 The Mews Cottages, the decision was aided by the smell of freshly ground coffee, just winning over the clean fragrance of peppermint, helped by the crackling log fire in the sitting area. And the oak beams in the bedrooms.

When we moved in, we noticed the odd damp patch, previously concealed by furniture, and the peppermint scent became more pervasive, but Handel looked very happy in his new home, and Nicole hummed a jaunty air as she flitted about placing this here and that there. I admit I liked the place.

What I did not like was having to get up in the middle of the first night when there was a loud crash from downstairs. Handel lay in pieces on the flags.

Nicole didn't hum on day two. She replaced Handel with a vase of flowers. Red ones, I think they were.

Second night, another crash. More mess on the flags.

On day three, I came back from shopping for some inessentials to find Nicole pointing to a chair at the table and holding a finger to her lips. I interpreted this as meaning sit and shut up. There was silence for a while.

Nicole broke it. 'There is a presence,' she said. 'A definite presence. The peppermint smell in connected, I'm sure.'

'And the breakages?' I asked.

'Of course. We must find a Psychic.'

'What? Now?' I protested. 'I've just come in. I need coffee.'

Deirdre Carrion, Psychic Medium, came that afternoon, demanded our birth dates and places, and then sat bolt upright on a hard chair for fifteen minutes.

When she came to, she said her spirit guide told her the niche was in fact a portal, a place of ingress and egress to and from somewhere vague. She muttered obliquely about "another dimension". Nicole asked if the beings, if beings there were, were spirits of light or of dark. Ms Carrion said her guide did not know those words. There were some questions that could not be asked.

Deirdre Carrion, Psychic Medium, then drank a cup of tea, ate three bourbon biscuits, accepted a large financial donation "in notes of the realm, if you please," and departed.

I managed to purchase a motion sensor security camera before the shops closed. When we went to bed, I set it up pointing towards the now empty niche.

We slept uninterrupted. In the morning, I fully expected to find the camera had not been triggered. I was wrong. At 2.15 am, the back of the niche had swung open, a concealed door, opening out into the room. Undoubtedly it was this motion that had swept Handel and the flowers to destruction.

Then something came out of the doorway very fast and shot out of view. It stayed invisible most of the time, but there was one sequence where it appeared on a low table next to the niche, on which Nicole had left her handbag. With clinical precision, the creature went through everything in the bag, flicking through her diary, inspecting her credit cards. It was all examined, then put back, except for pens, which the creature secreted away in some sort of pocket.

Just as it finished, it seemed to notice the camera. It waved a bony little hand at it and leaped. The picture went black. It remained that way for half an hour or so, then the motion sensor switched it off.

I looked at the camera closely. There was a sticky lump on top of the lens. Undoubtedly chewing gum. Peppermint flavour.

What did the creature look like? Hard to say. Infra-red images make things look unreal, but I reckon it had pointy ears and a mohican. Fingers long and thin. Big eyes that, in that moment it looked at the camera, seemed to speak of intelligence and mischief. And a grinning mouth, forever chewing, chewing.

During day five, I resolved to spend the night in that room. I set up a table light to provide a discrete light on the niche, and arranged a comfortable chair at a distance to give me good view while remaining inconspicuous. A glass of scotch at my elbow and I was all set.

At 2.15 I was awoken by the sound of a box of matches that I had deliberately left in the niche hitting the floor.

There was the creature looking at me. It grinned, picked its nose, adopted a nonchalant pose and spoke. The voice was high and rasping but intelligible.

'Yo man,' it said. 'Like the haircut?'

In the dim light, I could see it was indeed a mohican, and bright vermilion.

'What are you?' I asked in a whisper.

'Just one cool dude who needs a drink,' it cried, and in a couple of bounds it was beside me and the scotch had vanished down its throat.

'Wow, man,' it said. 'That was some vintage. Word of wisdom, sucker.' It leaned over so that I could smell the scotch on its breath. 'You are not alone. Don't think you are.'

And with that it was back in the niche and gone, the door closed and all but undetectable.

The next day, day six, I paid over the odds for a builder to drop what he was doing and come and brick up the niche.

And on the seventh day, the aroma of peppermint was gone. But then, so were all the remaining pens in the house. And I was sure I could now detect a distinct note of eucalyptus oil in the region of the sink's plug-hole.

Going on

This is Montague Lamb, known as Monty to his friends. He doesn't have many friends. Monty is a Yeoman Warder, or "Beefeater" to the common man. He works at the Tower, protecting the crown jewels. Correction. He used to work there. He is currently on indefinite leave pending psychiatric assessment.

'The trouble began,' Monty says, 'when I heard voices early one morning in the main display room. There aren't usually any visitors at that time, leastways not on a Monday in February. The voices sounded a bit weird-like, though they were perfectly comprehensible. "It's not easy being a National Treasure," said one, sounding thin and reedy. "Tell me about it," said the other voice, hollow, like it was speaking from inside a tin can or something. "All right," said the first, and commenced to do so at length. I could not stop to listen, being as how I am reprimanded if I loiter in one spot for too long a period, but when I returned that way some time later, the voice was still going on, going on about responsibilities and not being properly appreciated, and the need to keep up appearances, and how important its role was.

'I reckon that's where the trouble started. When someone says "Tell me about it," they actually mean "*Don't* tell me about it, I don't want to know." If you proceed to tell them anyway, they can get a bit uppity, do you know what I mean? And that's what happened here, in my opinion. Why are you frowning?'

This catches the assessing psychoanalyst out, because she is convinced her facial expressions are entirely devoid of nuance, utterly impartial. Maybe Monty is hypersensitive. That would fit.

'Go on,' she says.

'Well,' Monty continues, 'I kept hearing this conversation continuing over the next few days, each time becoming more and more of an argument. Always in the same place in the same display room. Always when there were no visitors around. I was perplexed, let me tell you. It was just in front of a case containing some of the main coronation regalia: St Edward's Crown, the 12 century gold anointing spoon, the orb, the sceptre and so on. I thought I was going bonkers.'

He looks at the analyst. She adopts her most deadpan of deadpan faces. *I should have been a poker player*, she thinks.

'Go on,' she says.

'Well, anyway,' Monty says, 'it must have been a week or so later, by which time the voices had become really heated, when I suddenly heard "Hey you!" I looked around. There was nobody. "Yes you," it went on, "you with the silly hat and wearing a skirt. We want you to give us an unbiased opinion." I have to tell you, doctor... should I call you doctor?' he asks.

'Go on,' she says.

'Well then, I have to tell you that I'm proud of my uniform. It is venerable. It is not a skirt. It is a tunic. And the hat is not silly. Not in any way, shape or form. Call me a sentimental old traditionalist if you like...'

'Go on,' she says.

'Well, I bit my tongue and swallowed my pride, and said "Are you addressing me?" in my most pompous voice. And the voice – it was the hollow echoey voice – said "Yes, you. To whom else would we be speaking?" There being no other person about, I could see the point, but then... who were they? "Excuse me asking," I said, "but who are you?"

'"I'm the f'ing Royal Orb, you numbskull, religious symbol representing the Monarch's role as Defender of the Faith and as Supreme Governor of the Church of England. And this useless, argumentative and entirely misguided upstart is the Sceptre." "The Royal Sceptre, If you don't mind" said the reedy voice, "symbolic ornamental rod borne in the hand by a ruling monarch as an item of royal or imperial insignia." I looked at the orb and sceptre. There they were, in their snug case of bullet-proof glass, no mouths that I could see, and yet I could hear them as clear as I can hear you, miss.'

The analyst sighs – but only internally. 'Go on,' she says.

'Well, the two of them were clearly overwrought and emotional. "There you are," said the Orb, "Completely delusional. The Sceptre is nothing but pointless, unnecessary trapping, and makes the Monarch look idiotic." "But," said the Sceptre, "I look far more prepossessing than a ball with a cross on top. And the Monarch, may she live for ever, can always hit someone with me. You are a mere encumbrance. And awkward to hold," he added with a sniff.

'"See what I mean," cried the Orb. "That's what it's all about. We want your opinion, pathetic mortal that you are. Which of us is the more worthy?" Well now, doctor miss, which would you have chosen?'

The psychoanalyst looks at her watch, and crosses her legs the other way because one foot is beginning to go numb. Time for coffee and a fig roll in ten minutes, she thinks. 'Go on,' she says.

'Well now, you – I said to the Sceptre – are statuesque, and holding you would look authoritative. I'm thinking of conductor's batons, schoolmasters' canes, sergeant majors' swizzle sticks, that sort of thing. I can see all that. But a ball. I turned to the Orb. Might look a bit like a bomb, but that's all. No, it looks to me like the Sceptre definitely got it nailed.

'"I see," said the resonant voice of the Orb. "So that's what the common man thinks, is it? Are you," it cried, and I felt if it had a hand it would be jabbing a finger at me, "aware of the issue of refreshment? Have you given a moment's thought to how long the coronation ceremony is?" And at that the top of the orb slowly began to rise. I was agog, doctor, I'm telling you straight. And do you know what was inside?'

Monty pauses dramatically. The analyst, who is beginning to think this assessment is as interminable as a coronation, finds she actually does want to know. 'Go on,' she says, with feeling this time.

'A chocolate orange, as I live and breathe, doctor. A genuine Terry's chocolate orange. Do you know the things, doctor.'

'Yes, yes,' she says, in spite of herself, the yearning for the fig roll becoming irresistible.

Monty repeats, 'A chocolate orange. Well, the case was clear. The Orb is the winner, I cried. Absolutely no doubt. The Orb is not just symbolic. It is actually useful as well!

'It was at that moment that I realised I was being watched. One of my fellow Yeomen Warders and the Chief Warder were standing in the doorway and looking at me very strangely.

'And that, doctor miss, is why I was suspended from duties, and why I am here today.' Monty folds his arms and looks at her.

The psychoanalyst puts her pad and pen down and meets his gaze. 'You do go on, don't you' she says, in spite of herself. 'Time for a break, I think.'

The Third Age

Ants in the Pants

It was a day of disquiet. Edith felt uneasy, unable to settle to anything. After breakfast, she went out into the garden, secateurs in hand, with good intentions, but apart from trimming an odd errant twig here and there, failed to do anything useful. Slugs continued their morning lettuce undisturbed, aphids sucked the sap out of the nasturtiums unsquashed, the black spot rampaged through the roses unchallenged. Perseus, her cat, hid behind the agapanthus and watched Edith warily. Eventually Edith would go in for coffee, he knew, and read her book, and he would have a bit of decent rest on her lap.

She went in, but then started scouring bookshelves, picking things out, glancing at them, putting them back. The coffee went cold, the lap remained on the move. Perseus felt the disquiet acutely.

Lunch was baked beans on toast. Cold baked beans. It seemed Edith was distracted. She ate them without showing any signs of distaste. She paid little attention to the Archers' repeat, where normally she relished savouring the tedious contrivances of her surrogate family for a second time.

Nonetheless, she then pulled her bike out of the shed and pedalled off to her clay modelling class as was customary on a Tuesday afternoon. Perseus breathed a sigh of relief and settled down on her chair for a proper sleep.

Edith was working on a model cottage, with roses round the door, a thatched roof, a tiny garden, and a little old lady sitting on a bench. She had worked on it for several weeks now, and it was not far off being ready to be fired. She lifted the cloth off the sculpture and gazed upon her handiwork. The clay seemed listless, overworked, crude, devoid of expression. As Edith looked, she realised that the lumpy figure on the bench was her. She had portrayed herself, and she was lifeless. A dollop of clay.

Without thinking, she grasped the figure and squeezed hard. Then she leant down on the cottage and its roses, so that it buckled and collapsed.

Cynthia, the tutor, was at her shoulder. 'Edith!' she cried.

'It won't do!' said Edith, and she wasn't talking about the clay model.

Edith mounted her bike and cycled off through the town. She went to Tesco's. Nothing odd in that, except that she didn't leave her bike outside. She cycled towards the doors, which obediently opened for her. She cycled past the fruit and veg, momentarily bathed in light designed to make items look fresh and appetising. She wobbled round the corner to pass the meat counter, giving the nice young man with his straw boater a wave as she passed. Her attempts to grab a sample of ham from a little dish on the counter only succeeded in knocking it on the floor, but on she went, past the bakery section, savouring the glorious aroma. She rounded another corner and collided with a shopper's trolley. 'Sorry!' she said as she slid to the floor, but undaunted, she picked herself and the bike up and was off again.

By this time, there was a little commotion brewing among the stores' shelf-stackers and checkout operatives. Their training, at least what little they could remember of it, had not covered little old ladies on bicycles, so they lacked direction and failed to muster a cohesive strategy.

By the time Edith sailed past and out of the doors again, they had only got as far as gawping and yelling a bit.

Edith felt a lot better. Out in the open air, a flush suffused her cheeks and determination inflated her spirit. She sailed, on, defying minor inconveniences like red lights, leaving confusion behind her, but, luckily, no carnage. She sailed on until she reached that great Gothic pile, that pillar to the spiritual health of the townsfolk, the Cathedral.

Her entrance was not entirely grand. She had to come to a halt to try to open the door and manoeuvre herself and her bike through, an awkward and undignified operation. But once inside, the space called to her, and she hopped along to mount her steed and sped off down aisles and nave, rejoicing in the space and the light and the ambience. There was quite a sprinkling of visitors in the cathedral. They gawped like the supermarket operatives.

And the great building filled Edith with glory and something bubbled up through her and emerged as… As Song! While she pedalled around she sang. *'The hills are alive,'* she burst out, her voice thirty years younger and strong and vibrant. *'The hills are alive with the sound of music!'* It echoed round the vaulted roof. *'With songs they have sung for a thousand years.'* The words came back to her. It was so appropriate, it was so infectious, this funny old lady beaming and carolling and cycling round in circles. Some of the visitors, caught up, joined in. *'My heart wants to sing every song it hears,'* they chorused, and the cathedral responded.

By the time the verger and other cathedral staff mobilised themselves to try to take action, the visitors were completely entranced and solidly defended the anarchic cyclist. While they and the verger argued, Edith sailed off into the afternoon, and arrived back home, still singing.

She made a cup of tea, and took it and a biscuit into the garden, where she sat on her garden bench, and

Perseus sat on her lap, and the sun shone, and the slugs and aphids and birds all carried on unmolested, and all was right with the world.

Pontin

Joan, the Major and I decided to take a stroll on the terraces after dinner. The sun was just setting, rather gloriously. The Major was so stirred by it he started reciting a chunk of poetry, when Joan cried, 'Hello, what's this?'

We turned to see a figure approaching from the house on the upper terrace. Although it was silhouetted against the sky, it was immediately recognisable as Pontin, the butler. The bearing, the gliding gait, all indicated so.

As he neared, he said, 'Excuse me interrupting, madam, gentlemen, but there is a telephone call for Major Carstairs. If you would care to take it in the library, sir, the caller did express a sense of urgency...'

Joan interrupted. 'Pontin, you are floating in mid-air.'

Pontin glanced down. He raised an eyebrow and gently descended to the ground. 'My apologies, madam,' he said. 'The upper terrace used to extend further out. Major, if you please...'

He led the Major away.

'Well,' said Joan. 'I am not accustomed to such behaviour. Hovering in mid-air, whatever next?'

'It was indeed curious,' I said. 'Although a butler, Pontin does appear to be flesh and blood as you and me, but perhaps gravity does not apply to his class of person.'

'On the contrary,' Joan said, 'I have observed members of the lower classes lying prone in the gutter outside drinking establishments in town. They did not float. I was passing by in an automobile, I hasten to add.'

'So, if immunity to gravity is not the explanation,' I said, 'where does that leave us?'

We took a turn around a bed boasting a delicate Japanese maple underpinned with lupins, in order to contemplate this odd state of affairs.

'Pontin does glide,' I observed. 'But he still appears to be in contact with the floor, at least in the house. I assumed gliding was something one was taught at butling school.'

'As a horse is taught to trot,' added Joan. 'Just so. It occurs to me...'

'Yes?'

'No, it is too impossible.'

She aroused my curiosity. 'Go on, Joan. I promise I won't laugh.'

'Well,...' she drew a long breath. 'You described Pontin as flesh and blood. Suppose he is not.'

It was getting quite dark now. What was she driving at? I shivered involuntarily. 'You mean...' I began.

'I don't know what I mean,' she said. 'Let us go in.'

That seemed to be that. She said nothing more until we were inside. Then she announced, 'I shall retire to my room. Tell the maid to bring my camomile tea and cognac up when nightcaps are served.' And off she went.

I wandered into the drawing room, where several others were, chatting, reading, generally letting time pass. Could I introduce the subject of Pontin floating in mid-air without appearing to be raving mad? What after all did I know of butlers? I assumed they did things like eating and sleeping. They presumably had parents and childhoods and so on, possibly even feelings. But it was all supposition. They could be robots for all I knew. I resolved to watch Pontin closely thenceforward.

The Major came in. At least I could talk to him; he had been there, he had seen.

'Major,' I said, 'what do make of that Pontin business?'

'It's no good,' he replied. 'They're going to put the old fellow down. Tried everything. It would cost a fortune to operate and would only give him another month or two at the outside. And no more jumping. So best thing. Bit of a blow. The old chap's been like a chum to me.'

I realised he was talking about one of his horses. Must have been the vet on the phone. I wasn't going to get much sense out of him over Pontin.

At that moment however, the butler himself entered, bearing a tray of glasses and a decanter of port. I watched eagle-eyed. He placed them on the sideboard. It all seemed wholly normal. He turned to leave, and walked – all right, it was a gliding sort of walk, but a walk nonetheless – to the door, opened it and went out.

And then...

That door has quite a strong spring. I swear, I would stand up in a court of law and swear, that the door closed before Pontin was entirely through. It closed through him, as though he was...

There. I must say it. As though he was a ghost, a spectre.

Of a sudden, I began to doubt everything. Was I living in a world of make-believe? Forget fake news, this was about fake people. Who was real? Was this person or that person merely a phantasm of someone who used to be? The very foundations of my beliefs trembled.

I headed for the port. Any port in a storm. It tasted good and wholesome, but at least, like a solid rock in the midst of a sea of uncertainty, at least I knew for sure it wasn't a spirit.

Single Malt

'Call me old, call me deaf, but I heard every word this old duffer said, before he went completely gaga, of course.' My uncle indicated a man with a jutting jaw and a fine moustache slumped in the next chair, who was dribbling a little.

'Fitzwalter, that's his name. Colonel Fitzwalter. It was in the war. His chaps had requisitioned Chervil Hall, do you know it? Fine old house. And Fitzwalter here set up his HQ in the library, among the first editions and whatnot.

'Then one day, this fellow appears, from where, he had no idea. Short, hairy chap with a face like a wrinkled prune. Said he'd come for his Glenfiddich. Fitzwalter told him to buzz off, and the chap went berserk. F'ing and blinding, screaming that Lord Chervil had always had a bottle of Glenfiddich handy, and if Fitzwalter knew what was good for him, he'd get some in toot suite. And the little man stomped off, God knows where.

'Anyway, a few days later, Fitzwalter was talking with a big noise from the War Office when this little hairy chap pops up again, as from nowhere, and starts insulting the War Office chappie. Said he'd a face like a baboon's bottom and probably thought soldiers were what you dipped into a boiled egg.

'War Office man stormed out, highly offended. Fitzwalter livid. Little hairy chap says, "Where's me Glenfiddich?"

'Well, after a few embarrassing episodes like this, Fitzwalter marches off to the mess and demands a bottle of Scotch. Now the Colonel is a sherry man, would you believe. Takes all sorts, I suppose. Anyway, he didn't appreciate the finer qualities of single malts, so, of course, they gave him a cheap blend. It was wartime, after all.

'Next time the little blighter appears, he thrusts the bottle of Scotch at him. "Take it and clear off," he says. Smoke comes out of the hairy chap's ears, he lets out a blood-curdling scream, dives under the desk, and starts gnawing away at Fitzwalter's ankles. Fitzwalter pulls out his revolver and lets off round after round, perforating God knows how many priceless first editions.

'When they found him later, he was a gibbering wreck. The little chap had done so much damage, they had to amputate a foot. Packed him off to the loony bin. That's this place here, wouldn't you know. Called a Retirement Home for Gentlemen now, and you don't have to be bonkers to live here. Helps though. He's been here forty years. I'm the only one who takes his stories seriously.'

At that moment, a door opened, and a small, bearded wizened man stomped in bearing a tray with two glasses and a bottle of Glenfiddich. He poured a generous tot into each glass, presented one to my uncle, and downed the other himself. In one.

'That'll do, Boggart,' said my uncle.

The little chap bowed, winked, said 'Very good, Lord Chervil,' and vanished, pfft, just like that.

Something to Do

Gwilym had an earworm, a tune going round and round in his head. An irritating tune. He said, 'I'll take my coffee up with me.'

Ethyl carried on reading the paper. Gwilym sighed, and started up the stairs. As he neared the attic, he heard sounds, as of a tinny purring, and smelled a faint whiff of ozone.

'Blast,' he thought. Under the skylight, the passenger train was merrily running backwards. It must have been going all night. This had happened before, though he was sure he was always careful to turn it off last thing.

Out of the corner of his eye, he caught a flicker, a coruscation over by the controller. The moment he looked directly at it there was nothing.

The train was still rumbling around. Gwilym reached over to the controller to stop it. As he moved the lever, he felt an excruciating pain. He looked at his hand, where the fleshy side of his palm was beginning to ooze blood. It looked very like a bite mark.

Downstairs, Ethyl was wandering about waving a duster. 'Where are the plasters?' asked Gwilym. 'I've cut myself.'

Ethyl made scornful clicking noises. 'In the drawer.'

Gwilym went into the kitchen.

'In the bathroom!' shouted Ethyl.

He washed the wound. It was definitely a bite. He stuck on a plaster, and looked at himself in the mirror. His eyes looked tired. He began the train layout when he retired to give himself something to do. He liked model railways. If they'd had a son...

The tune in his head, his earworm, carried on repeating. Four bars of six-eight. Trite. There were words, but he couldn't put his finger on them. Could things like that drive you mad? His eyes gazed back at him wearily.

He returned to the attic. It seemed quiet now, but the magic of the place, that other world into which he escaped, had no appeal now, not this morning with his hand throbbing and that bloody tune. He decided to look at the paper while he finished the coffee.

'You can't stay here,' said Ethyl as he sat down. 'I always do downstairs on a Tuesday as you very well know.'

Of course. It was Tuesday. He wasn't too sure what "doing downstairs" actually meant, apart from the stipulation that he shouldn't clutter the place up while she was doing it. Downstairs always looked exactly the same afterwards. But it wasn't his place to argue. It was softly raining outside. Nevertheless, he put on his coat and went out.

His pace kept time with the infernal earworm. "Diddledy diddledy pom, pom, diddledy diddledy pom."

Where was he going? The library. He could go there. Read the paper until time for elevenses. The Art Gallery next to the library had a new exhibition on: "Performance and Art". Outside on the pavement was a piano bedecked with flowers. A young woman was standing by it.

'Want a go?' she asked him.

Gwilym could think of many reasons why he shouldn't. He hadn't touched a piano since he was married. It was drizzling. He would feel self-conscious and look silly. So he said 'Yes, please,' and sat on the wet stool and opened the lid.

And without him touching a note, it played by itself – a bright and breezy tune, a tune he recognised.

The girl was laughing. 'Your expression,' she said. 'It takes everyone by surprise!'

'What is that piece?' asked Gwilym.

'It's from Salad Days. *"I'm looking for a piano..."*'

Gwilym smote himself on the forehead. 'Of course it is,' he cried, and found himself singing along.

'Thank you so much,' he said to the girl when it finished. 'Look! It's made the rain stop!'

'Come and see the exhibition,' she said.

'Later on,' he said. 'I'm off to the park.' Somehow he felt the need to sit for a while among flowers and trees.

The park benches were wet, but he didn't care. A squirrel dashed about in stop-motion animation. And suddenly a realisation struck him: the earworm, that was from Salad Days too. The words came to him:

"Find yourself something to do, dear,
Find yourself something to do."

Young Timothy, fresh out of University, being offered career choices by four uncles and the piano making everyone dance, and the final lines:

"If you should happen to find me
With an outlook dreary and black,
I'll remind you to remind me
We said we wouldn't look back."

And of a sudden, whatever it was that was going on with his model railway, he knew what he had to do.

Bidding the squirrel adieu, Gwilym went home, surprising Ethyl, who was watching a shopping programme with her feet up and a box of chocolates. He found a hand mirror and mounted to the attic, where the train was ambling round the track again.

This time, instead of looking directly, he turned around and looked at the reflection of the layout in the mirror, and there at the controller, he could see a small creature like a little punk rocker, with a bright vermilion crest of hair, trousers worn impossibly low and a wicked grin. On the trundling train sat another, sticking two fingers up to him.

As he watched in the mirror, a taller, more sober-looking creature appeared, slapped the two punks about the head, and towed them away back into the dark recesses of the attic.

After a moment, Gwilym turned round and stopped the train. There, by the controller, was a scrap of paper.

He picked it up and read, in tiny letters, "Sorry. Won't happen again."

Then he went downstairs and suggested to Ethyl that she might like to look at an art exhibition with him, and they might perhaps have lunch out afterwards.

She looked flabbergasted. 'Well,' she said, sniffing, 'I suppose it'll give us something to do.'

Don't Count Your Chickens

It is reassuring when there's someone already there at the bus-stop. At least your understanding that a bus will come along in the foreseeable future is shared, even if it turns out to be the wrong bus. There are two of them there, one with a brolly, the other with one of those things like a pleated bit of plastic bag that you put over your head and tie with strings under your chin. I don't have anything to keep the rain off, but then I'm bald, so what's the need? Let nature wash my cranium for me.

'You want the 27, dearie?' asks the plastic bag.

'No,' I say, 'the X2.'

'That's a good thing,' she says. 'The 27's just been and gone. You're like me, ducks, lucky. I can tell.' She taps the side of her nose.

'Blessed rain,' says the umbrella. I can't tell if she is complimenting or cursing the drizzle.

The first lady sniffs. I reckon she's in her eighties, but her twinkly eye makes her seem youthful, and makes up for one stocking being bunched around her ankle. 'I'm going to buy a house,' she tells me.

'That's nice,' I say.

'More like a mansion, probably. Like them footballers and pop stars have. With a swimming pool and that.'

I try to imagine her reclining by her own pool, Sanatogen tonic wine in hand, James Last burbling away on a gramophone.

The umbrella lady clicks her tongue and purses her lips. 'Don't be telling every Tom, Dick and Larry, Edna. They'll all be pestering you, mark my words.'

'Don't you worry, Doris. This one's all right. He's no scrounger. Not with that nose. I can tell.' Edna's eye twinkles overtime.

'What's wrong with my nose,' I demand. It is perfectly acceptable as noses go, I think.

'It's dripping, dearie.'

'That's the rain,' I protest. 'Any nose would drip.'

She looks momentarily crestfallen, and then rallies. 'That's as may be, sonny, but noses are critical.'

'Critical,' echoes Doris from under her umbrella.

'That's what I says,' says Edna. 'Critical. That's why I'm buying a mansion. Should I have stables and that?' she asks Doris.

'Up to you,' says Doris. 'Do you like horses?'

'Not specially,' Edna announces. 'Take them or leave them, me. It's the look of the thing. Gives a mansion a bit of balance, if you ask me. Something to set off the terraces and croquet lawn and what-not. Should I have a live-in gardener, do you think?'

Doris grunts non-committally. Something is troubling me.

'Forgive me,' I say, 'but you don't look, how can I put it, the mansion-buying type.'

Edna glares. 'Just cos I'm not a footballer nor a duchess nor nothing. Money, young man, is money, whether you is the Queen or Edna Sparrow. 'Ere, do you know a good Estate Agent in Chervil, sonnie? Not your run-of-the-mill, something Town and County like?'

'You could try Fudge and Fleasom in Broad Street,' I suggest, 'if you've a couple of million to splash around.' I laugh at my little joke. Edna is not amused.

'That's insulting, dearie. I'm looking at more like twenty or thirty million, I reckon. I was never good at sums. Close your mouth, ducks, I can see your fillings.'

Doris explains, 'It's her nose, that's what she says.'

Edna carries on. 'That's right, my nose. I'm winning them what-d'you call it...'

'Lottery thing,' fills in Doris.

'EuroMillions,' Edna says. 'That's what. Roll over something. Lots of millions. Soon as I bought me ticket, I knew. It's in my nose, see. I can always tell.'

I see a flaw in all this. 'You've not actually won them yet?' I ask.

'Good as,' she says. 'My nose says so.'

I go on, 'And you're going to spend them before you've got them? On a mansion?'

'Why not, sonnie? You can't take them with you. Should I go for somewhere with a ballroom and an escarpment, Doris?'

Doris winces. 'You mean an *escritoire*, Edna. Escarpments are what you have in watches.'

At which the X2, express by nomenclature but not by nature, draws up, spraying our legs from a puddle by the bus stop.

Edna and Doris flash their bus passes, and as I pay for my ticket, I catch sight of them ejecting a very pregnant woman from the seats for the elderly and infirm, though the bus is otherwise empty.

I sit near the back because I always do.

When we reach the centre, Edna and Doris, surprisingly nimble, are off first. By the time I reach the door, they are lying in wait, one each side. They catch my arms and off we go, into the crowds.

I watch us vanish, a strange sandwich, a polished cranium like an egg between two little bundles with brolly and plastic rain-hood, and I wonder how I can still be standing here watching, when that's me disappearing down the street. And yet there I am, and here I am. In a moment we, or is it they?, are out of sight. I sneeze and blow my nose. It isn't just rain. I'm definitely getting a cold. Must have caught a chill. Blessed rain.

Later on, for me after coffee and before M&S, I see them again. What is between Edna and Doris is more like an old raincoat, with barely a body inside, only the polished egg, dripping with rain, poking out of the top. I seem to have shrivelled up. I don't confront them, because I am on a mission to buy some underpants. I wonder if they'll catch the same bus back.

And indeed they do. At least Edna and Doris do.

'Did you buy a mansion?' I ask.

Edna looks sly. 'No, dearie,' she says, 'I didn't like the colours they had. So I bought this.' She ferrets in a capacious handbag and produces what looks like a hen's egg.

'It looks like an egg,' I say.

She sniffs. 'Looks ain't everything,' she says, and taps her nose in that conspiratorial way. She waves the egg. 'This is going to be my little pet, sweetheart. Wait till it hatches. Worth more than mansions. My nose says so, and it's never wrong.' She winks at me, removes her rain-hood and tries to fold it up. In the process she fumbles awkwardly. And drops the egg...

Home To Go To

The fire sings softly to itself, glowing with health and ruddy cheeks, cackling in spits like an old crone. Nobody is left in the bar apart from the regulars. All men bar one, in their regular places, drinking their regular drinks. Although they all have homes to go to, Jim, the landlord is about to question that anyway.

There at the bar, at the end, Fender, side-whiskers full of old country wisdom fashioned from cider. Next to him is Rita, maybe 40, maybe 80, mostly rouge and powder applied with a shaking hand that leaves her ghost-like and haggish. Next to her, Merv, retired stockbroker, lost his wife six months back and the Four Alls is her replacement. Next to him, the twins, either Eric and Derek or vice versa. Nobody knows. They never speak. And there in the inglenook, in the old high-backed church pew by the fire, Mr Gregory, ancient as granite, worn as a pebble.

They all sip and glug and sometimes a discussion breaks out, the price of beer, the state of the government, the validity of Papal accession, why there aren't as many flies now as when they were young – you never know what may arise. But often they sit in silence, and time passes. There is warm, rosy harmony. No-one judges them, though each is a judge of others.

Jim, the landlord, looks over them like a good shepherd. He's heard all their tales a thousand times, but he laughs at their jokes again and nods at their specious saws. And eventually, when the hour comes, he calls time.

'Time, gentlemen please,' he cries, 'gentlemen and Rita. Haven't you got homes to go to?'

And tonight, because it is the infernal equinox and Jim is the good shepherd, for once it really is time. Time for the regulars. As the fire crackles, they go to their final home and are at peace.

And tomorrow, or next week, or next month, after the funerals, Jim will cultivate a few new lost souls – the sad, the lonely, the tired. They will drift towards the Four Alls and start to prop up the bar. And in their own way, the fire, the crackling log, the beer and Jim will spread a little comfort and cheer and warmth, until once again, Jim sees the moment has arrived, and calls time.

Pink Bells

The pair progress laboriously along the path in the park. He's leaning on a stick, each step a pain, she's almost bent double, hand in his. She clutches a paper bag. They sit carefully on a bench, very close, avoiding the damper spots. In front of them stretches a sea of pink bells.

It is nine in the morning, and the bag contains croissants. Ethel hands one to Arthur. They both nibble in silence, flakes fluttering from them like confetti.

After a while, while a blackbird sings and sparrows edge towards the crumbs, Ethel extends a bent finger towards a plaque half-submerged in the flowers.

'What does it say?' she asks.

'I don't know,' he says, because it is several feet away and his eyes aren't too good.

With a groan, she manages to get to her feet and shuffles towards it. Bent as she is, she still can't make it out. She retrieves a pair of spectacles hanging round her neck, and peers closer.

Arthur hears her saying something, but his hearing is not too good either. He sees her move forward among the flowers. As she does, she shrinks, smaller and smaller, until she vanishes into the pinkness.

Two sparrows squabble over a croissant crumb and fly off, startling Arthur. He struggles to rise. With his stick, he moves the blooms aside so that he can see the plaque clearly. He expects something like the botanical name and the English common name of the plant, or perhaps the name of a business which has sponsored this bed, but it simply says 'Come in. Make yourself at home.'

So he steps into the sea of flowers, and at once the pink bells inflate and grow until they are several times his height. The scent is overwhelming, the chime of the bells deep and sonorous. He walks towards Ethel and the others, finding himself praying that it doesn't rain. A raindrop the size of a settee would be unsettling. But, he thinks, they must have ways of dealing with that.

Back on the bench, a little breeze sweeps the paper bag off into a graceful dance, a homage, an obeisance, and all is still.

about the author

I used to write Computer User Manuals, but having retired, now prefer to replace writing facts that nobody reads with producing whimsical fiction that people can enjoy. I live in Abergavenny, which should be known as the Rome of Wales, because it has seven hills and a few Roman remains.

In a previous existence as a Maths teacher, I wrote and directed two full-length plays, and I've composed a number of musical pieces, mostly for choir, which have received performances in widely-flung places around the world. They are freely available from my web-site, *www.musicolib.net*, or through the Choral Public Domain Library (ChoralWiki – *www.cpdl.org/wiki/*).

In my writing, I seek to bring a wry touch to the commonplace activities of everyday life – "in the ordinary is the extraordinary." Frequently, angels and bad-tempered mythical beings such as garden gnomes creep in, despite my best endeavours. Hence **Away with the Fairies**, where they have generally taken over.

I'm currently working on novels set in the fictional small city of Chervil. The first, **Mouse**, is published simultaneously with **Away with the Fairies**. It tells of 57-year old Brian Ellis, culinary antiquarian bookseller, and how he faces the challenge of becoming a vaguely confident and socially ept person after a lifetime of belittling by his late mother. He is a mouse. His coming-of-age involves a small group of amateur restaurant critics, a cat, and a lot of eating and drinking. And the question of who is, or was, Dolores? It too is published by The Deri Press.

The second novel, **Creation**, explores the problems of creation, if the creations come to life and plague you. It is set against the preparations for a performance of Haydn's Creation by the local choral society and orchestra. Coming soon to The Deri Press!

Oliver Barton
oliver.barton@talktalk.net

Lightning Source UK Ltd.
Milton Keynes UK
UKHW010622291122
413042UK00001B/95

9 781739 158927